You Must Remember This

KAREN L. B. EVANS AND PAT DADE

HYPERION BOOKS FOR CHILDREN
NEW YORK

PRINTED IN THE UNITED STATES OF AMERICA.

First Edition

1 3 5 7 9 10 8 6 4 2

Evans, Karen L. B.
You must remember this / Karen L. B. Evans and Pat Dade. — 1st ed.
p.   cm.
Summary: A class assignment to make a video excites ten-year-old Ella,
who wants to become a filmmaker like her Great-uncle Buddy.
ISBN 0-7868-0090-9 (trade) — ISBN 0-7868-2075-6 (lib. bdg)
[1. Motion pictures—Production and direction—Fiction.
2. Great-uncles—Fiction. 3. Afro-Americans—Fiction.]
I. Dade, Pat. II. Title.
PZ7.E8875Yo 1997
[Fic]—dc20
96-4242

For Cristina
*who inspired Ella's ten-year-old
laugh, wit, and imagination*
—K. L. B. E.

For Amber
who already loves movies as much as I do
—P. D.

SCENE 1

Fade In: *When the movie begins, the screen is dark. The screen slowly becomes lighter, revealing the very first picture of the movie.*

"Faaaaade innnn," I whispered to myself.

Faaaaade innnn," I whispered to myself.

Sitting at the top of the steps, I could see most of the TV screen down in the living room. If I stayed really quiet, Mom and Dad wouldn't even know I was here.

The TV went black. I heard a crack of thunder, and a bolt of lightning lit up the screen. The words STORMY WEATHER appeared. I moved forward just a little bit and heard the wooden step creak.

"Go to bed, Ella," my mom called.

"I don't know why she thinks she's invisible up there at the top of the stairs," said my dad as he came into the living room.

Rats, I thought. I stomped loudly back to my room.

I lay across my bed and stared at my white lace curtain

1

rising and falling with the evening breeze. So much for the late movie. I'd have to make my own.

I hoisted my imaginary Canon ES-800 video camera—which I know my dad is going to buy for me someday, maybe next year for my eleventh birthday—onto my shoulder and began to shoot.

"Down the alley, hey, who is that . . . no, no, yes . . . it's me, Ella Jackson herself . . . and look at that girl go! Let's follow her with our camera!

"She's picked up a stick, clacking it along the wood fences, now chain-link, now wood again, of the row houses on Biltmore Street, then right—onto Columbia Road. The street, folks! The people, the action, the 'hood!

"She's passing stores like the Gap, with stonewashed jeans on flat plastic people, and Popeye's, with the red-and-yellow flashing sign.

"At Lorenzo's, someone's asleep at the table as usual. She waves to Ms. Montgomery, her neighbor. Then she strolls down to *Editorio el Mundo*, with newspapers from Spain to Ethiopia hanging on clotheslines, and buys the *Amsterdam News* for her Uncle Buddy.

"She's stopping at her Uncle Buddy's barbershop. Reading the CLOSED sign, she remembers it's night, and she takes off!

2

"Yes, folks, she's FLYING! Through the air! And you are there! Hear the *whoosh* as she cuts through the air, more graceful than a bird, faster than a 747. Over the lights of the night, over grown-ups out for dinner and a good time, teenagers trying to jam each other out with boom boxes playing salsa and rap. Over the rooftops, back to her house. Pan, zoom, close-up!"

I fell back on my bed, laughing. Now *that* was a great shoot. I love movies. Me and my great-uncle Buddy, who lives with us, are movie fan-a-tics!

I put my feet on the wall and let my head hang off the bed.

"Music," I thought. "If I were shooting my curtain, I would put chimes on the sound track. No . . . everybody expects that. How about music from that shark movie—*bum bum, bum bum*—faster, lower, the camera moves in. . . . You don't know who or what is coming through that window. . . ."

Thwack!

The sound sent me tumbling onto the floor, head over heels. I expected cold hands to close around my neck at any second. *Thwack! Thwack!* right under my window.

Realizing the intruder was still outside, I scrambled to

3

my knees, crawled to the window, and pulled up to peer over the edge of the windowsill.

Alphonso Green was outside, using the wall under my window as a backboard.

"Are you crazy?" I screamed in the loudest possible whisper. "My parents will hear you!"

Alphonso lived with his mom in the apartment building at the end of my block. We had the same baby-sitter and had been friends all the way through kindergarten. Then kids had started teasing us about being boyfriend and girlfriend, and that pretty much put a stop to our friendship.

Alphonso dribbled around my small, square, brick-paved yard, his fat, round body moving quickly. He bounced the ball off the wall of the wooden fence at the back of the house and then lobbed it up toward my window.

I ducked.

Alphonso laughed.

"Does your mom know you're out at almost nine o'clock?"

"I still have five minutes. But I came to tell you, Ms. Minnie Mouse . . . ," he said sarcastically.

I ducked down again, embarrassed to be seen in pajamas, let alone *Minnie Mouse* pajamas.

4

". . . that your days are numbered."

I gulped. I was scared. I wondered if Alphonso's mother knew where he was. Probably not. I squashed the idea that she would appear at my backyard gate with her hand on her hip to put Alphonso in his place and save my butt.

Besides, lately it seemed that every time I heard Mrs. Green she was fussing at Alphonso, and his eyes would roll up in his head like she was talking to him in a foreign language.

Things had changed. Alphonso used to be at home where he was supposed to be at nine o'clock on a school night and not in my backyard threatening me.

Hmm. No Mrs. Green. Just me, Alphonso, and one big score to settle.

Today I had beaten him at a not-so-friendly game of one-on-one basketball.

It had started at three o'clock. The halls were noisy at Bancroft Middle School as the kids hit their lockers. I put a dollar on top of the books I was taking home. It was my allowance money, the dollar I used every week for the midweek matinee at the Bella Vista Movie Theater. Uncle Buddy and I had a standing date at the Bella Vista.

As I turned to my right, a size $8\frac{1}{2}$ LA Lights slammed down on my books and my dollar. I looked up at Alphonso's face, painted with a grin, and knew I was about to be pushed too far. He grabbed my dollar and took off. I followed him.

Alphonso came to a stop on the playground, where the Posse had already started its regular after-school game of basketball. Alphonso had thought up that name for the fifth-grade boys. That—and the fact that he had grown three inches over the summer—made him their leader.

I slowed down, knowing this was going to be ugly, now that he was with the Posse and the rest of the class was right behind me. An audience was the last thing I needed. All I wanted was to get my dollar back and get to the Bella Vista for the 3:20 showing of *Glory*. I was going to be late—if I got there at all.

"Give me my money back, Alphonso!"

Alphonso turned and gave me a look that made me want to back up a few steps. "Hey, you want your money, here it is," he replied. He ambled toward me, the dollar in his outstretched hand. I reached for it. Jerk! He snatched it back and swerved around me.

"Missed it! You better get some glasses, Ella. Here it is."

I made another grab, missing it again. The laughter got louder. The Posse was wild. They had stopped their game of basketball to cheer Alphonso on. This was not going well. It was 3:15. I had to do something, and fast!

As I made my third grab for the dollar, I pivoted and knocked the basketball from under Akil Franklin's arm. Dribbling quickly, I got the ball under control and slowly circled Alphonso.

"You want to play keep-away, huh? How about some one-on-one? Ten points. If I win, I get my dollar back."

"If you lose?"

"You keep it."

I saw a moment of hesitation on his face. The girls, who knew I was the best basketball player in our gym class, started chanting "Ella! Ella! Ella!" Akil started up another cheer, "Kick her butt, Big A, kick her butt, hey, hey!" Alphonso had to go for it.

Be cool, I told myself. Even though I know I'm good, and even after going to summer basketball camp, I knew Alphonso wouldn't cut me any slack. It was all or nothing.

One of the members of the Posse blew a whistle. I dribbled, rolled around Alphonso, and threw the ball. It flew through the air to the hoop. A cheer from the crowd—the girls, anyway.

I stole a quick look at my watch. It was 3:25. The matinee had already started.

7

Thwop! That second spent thinking about the movie and not concentrating on the game cost me two points. Alphonso was now in the lead. I took a deep breath and, remembering all the moves my father had taught me and all the ones I had made up myself in gym class, I went for it.

Thwop! One after the other I quickly racked up ten points to Alphonso's four.

I had never seen a look like that on Alphonso's face. Sort of mad and hurt and confused, all at the same time. He looked at me like I had done him wrong, big-time, which for some reason made me even madder. I grabbed my dollar from his outstretched hand and ran to get my books and try to make the movie. I didn't even stop to enjoy the screaming and cheering from the girls.

Why did I feel like it was all my fault? He started it. He took my dollar.

Too bad for him that the Posse was there to witness his defeat. Too bad he didn't know that I practiced in the backyard with my dad every Saturday.

The very backyard he had now invaded.

Downstairs, the back porch light came on. In a flash, Alphonso was out the gate, leaving it creaking behind him.

I ducked, then carefully peered out. Great-uncle

Buddy was just closing the gate. I stared down at the full whiteness of his head. It was like a cotton ball moving in the dark. His skin was dark brown and, for as long as I could remember, his head had been covered with pure white, cottony hair.

When I was little, I would trace the folds and lines on his face as he lay sleeping on the couch. I'd make *putt-putt* noises as if my finger were a boat and the deep lines of his face were rivers and streams.

He turned back toward the house and peered up at my window.

"Kinda late for company, isn't it, Ella?"

"Shh! They'll hear you!"

"They're watching television in the parlor." Uncle Buddy used funny words like parlor because he was almost eighty-five.

"Alphonso's visit got anything to do with why you missed the matinee today?"

"No. Yes. Sort of."

"I like that Alphonso."

"You know, Uncle Buddy, I've been meaning to tell you how downright mean Alphonso can be at times. . . ."

"Hmmm. Good night, Ella."

"Hey, Uncle Buddy, how about a story?"

"No indeed, Miss."

"Aw, come on, a short one—'The Purple Blossom' or 'The Bull Doggers'? Pull up a lawn chair!"

"And get both of us in trouble? No sirree. You tell yourself one, you know them all by heart. Good night, Ella."

"Good night, Uncle Buddy." I yawned and plopped down on my bed. He was right, I did know them all. The only thing better than movies were Uncle Buddy's stories.

"Gertie Watkins got off the train with only one beat-up suitcase. Chicago was a long way from Dry Prong, Louisiana. . . ."

SCENE 2

Focus: *If the picture looks fuzzy, unclear, you focus by moving the projector or camera lens until the picture is sharp.*

"Remember," shouted Ms. Sewall, "you're my video cadets! Keep your eyes peeled and your lens in focus!"

I ran up the stone steps of Bancroft Middle School two at a time. Being in fifth grade meant I was allowed to use the main entrance. I loved the big circular window on the second landing.

Every time I came in these doors, I tipped my head back. I felt like Alice falling through the looking glass into a forest of green leaves and morning light.

Before I made it to the third-floor landing, Juanita, Debra, and Renee had surrounded me.

"Ooh, girl," said Renee, "I heard Alphonso is mad at you."

"Tell me something I don't know," I replied.

Debra grabbed my hand. "I heard him telling the Posse that he was going to be waiting for you on the playground. You know what that means."

Juanita hit her palm with a fist.

"I'm not afraid of him," I lied. "I'm not even thinking about him."

Throughout the day, I heard people whispering about me and Alphonso, but I refused to pay attention to the plans and counterplans of Alphonso's Revenge. Whatever he had in mind, I would just have to deal with it.

Every now and then I felt a spitball hit me in the neck. Or, as Alphonso was walking by me on his way to the blackboard, he would "accidentally" bump into my desk, or kick a book, or knock something to the floor.

I wanted the day to be over. I wished I were sitting at my desk in Uncle Buddy's barbershop doing my homework. Oh, no! What was I saying? If I'd rather be doing homework, man, this was a really bad day.

It was time for the geography lesson, but instead of telling us to take out our books, Mrs. Henderson made an announcement.

"Settle down, everybody! We have a visitor. I've just received a note saying that she's in the office, and I'm going to go get her. I want everybody to rest his or her head

12

while I'm gone. And I don't want to hear a peep when I get back here. Alphonso, take names." Groans came from the class, and mine must have been the loudest because Mrs. Henderson turned to me and said, "Do you have a problem with that, Ella?"

I slid down in my chair and mumbled, "But Mrs. Henderson, he's the one who's always starting something."

"With more than a little help from you, Ella. No more complaints. It's his turn."

There was a moment of silence after Mrs. Henderson left the room. It was showdown time, I decided. I had to face Alphonso sooner or later.

I walked to the middle of the room. Alphonso met me there.

We circled each other slowly.

Then I looked around the room, making sure I caught every kid's eye. "So . . . you guys want to hear one of my stories?" I asked. They all shouted, "YEEEEES!"

My stories are my ace. Well, Uncle Buddy's stories. Without them, I'd be, I don't know, just normal. My stories made me feel special. The kids loved them. Alphonso hated them.

"Those stories!" Alphonso growled. "You people act like you're in kindergarten, listening to her."

13

"You're just jealous because I can tell good stories."

"Stories, ha. Lies! Even Mrs. Henderson said, 'Ella, you have been known to stretch the truth.' Like the one about your Uncle Buddy being a movie star."

I bit my lip. Okay, so maybe Uncle Buddy wasn't a movie star, but he had been in a movie. Actually, I didn't know very much. Uncle Buddy never wanted to talk about it.

"How about the final chapter of 'Wild Bill Pickett and the Showdown at Boley'?" I asked.

I did a few wide warm-up stretches, elbowing Alphonso out of the way in the process.

"It was high noon at Boley," I began. "A dusty western town with a mean reputation. A town so mean, a man could get shot for snoring too loud. An all-colored town . . ."

"Colored? What color?" asked Manuel.

"That's what they called African Americans back then," I quickly explained. "And a stranger had come—a mean man in a white hat—and taken over the town. His name was Mad Dog Miller, and he was a killer.

"Nary a man, woman, child, or horse was to be found on the street. Would their friend, Wild Bill Pickett, the fastest gun in the West, come to save them?"

14

"Was he cute?" asked Yolanda. The girls giggled.

"You don't call cowboys cute, Yolanda," I said, trying not to sound annoyed. "Anyway, Wild Bill had been their friend, done right by them. Could he save them from the clutches of Mad Dog Miller? The bells in the old Baptist Church struck twelve. . . ."

"*Boing!*" yelled Alphonso, and he threw a paper airplane at me. It whizzed by closely. I slapped it down.

"I don't need your help," I said. "Tumbleweeds rolled by, then the sound of a horse. . . ."

The kids began patting their laps, imitating the sound of horses. I had them.

"Wild Bill Pickett was riding into town. The fastest gun in the Indian Territory. Faster than Billy the Kid, Doc Holliday, and Wyatt Earp all put together."

"Be for real," said Alphonso, folding another paper airplane.

"*Ssshh!*" came a voice from the back of the classroom. Alphonso looked, craning to see who had dared challenge him. It was Akil, a member of his own posse!

"So," I continued, moving slowly down the aisle, "Mad Dog Miller had been bragging that he was the fastest, the baddest cowboy around. When Wild Bill heard, well, he had no choice but to face Mad Dog. It was a matter of honor."

15

Another paper airplane whizzed by my face. Juanita, with her cornrow braids whipping in the air, and Denzel, taking off his Batman sunglasses, both stood up and yelled at Alphonso, "Cut it out!" at the same time. All eyes turned back to me.

It was time for the big finish.

"They stood there, facing each other."

I shifted my weight to one side, arms crossed over my chest, head tilted back, chin out. I was Wild Bill.

In a deep voice I said, "I hear you been lookin' fer me."

I shifted to the other side, hands on my hips, jaw stuck out and teeth showing, in imitation of Mad Dog Miller.

"Ay-yup," I said with an evil growl in my voice.

I shifted into my hero position. "I hear you think you're faster than me. Draw!"

I whipped an imaginary Colt .45 from my holster.

The class shouted, *"BANG! BANG! BANG!"*

I grabbed my stomach and, holding on to desks, knocking over books, slowly stumbled around the room.

"Mad Dog Miller, blood oozing from his gut, took one last look at Wild Bill Pickett, and knew he had been beaten by the best."

I dropped to the floor, kicked my feet up in the air and back down, and let out a long death rattle.

16

The class came out of their chairs, gathering around to stare down at me.

Manuel picked up my hand and let it go. I let it fall to the floor, like deadweight.

"Go 'head, girlfriend," said Juanita, totally impressed.

Every voice in the class—except Alphonso's—began quietly humming "Taps."

Eyes closed, I hummed along with them.

Suddenly I noticed I was the only one humming.

"Looks like there's been a murder, Mrs. Henderson," a woman's voice said.

My eyes popped open. I looked straight into Mrs. Henderson's frowning face. I froze. Next to her stood a tall, pretty woman with long, reddish dreadlocks. She gave me a wink.

"Ella Jackson," Mrs. Henderson began, "this is the last straw. I want you to—"

"Please," interrupted the woman. "Let me handle this. Please?" Mrs. Henderson threw her hands up and walked away.

The woman reached for my hand and began to take my pulse.

"*Hmmm.* No sign of life. This case looks like it could be a tough one to crack. I might need some help from kids

17

with sharp eyes who can notice detail and put together clues to solve a case. Any takers?"

One by one, the class began raising their hands. As the lady reached into her skirt pocket and began handing out buttons with little movie cameras on them, more hands went up.

"There," she said. "I'm Ricki Sewall, and you are now duly sworn video cadets, deputized to pursue truth, the beauty of film, and a really good story. Now, like all good detectives, I'm sure you've gathered some information. Time of death?"

Manuel quickly raised his hand and shouted, "Two-fifteen!"

"Good!" said Ms. Sewall. "Method of death?"

"Gunshot!" yelled Benny.

"Uh-huh. Type of weapon?"

"A six-shooter!" yelled Jonathan and Denzel together.

"Colt .45," I corrected.

"Ah, a very talkative corpse." She held out a hand to help me up.

"You're going to be spending your art periods with me in the new media center, in the big room on the second floor. Your parents have worked very hard the last year having bake sales and car washes to match grants for the cameras and editing equipment that you'll be using. And by the end of the semester, each and every one of you will have made a movie."

"A movie! We're going to make movies?" I shouted, jumping up and down.

"That's right, and you just got your first lesson in movie making."

"That was detective stuff," I said, a little confused. "We're going to make movies, not solve crimes, right?"

"True," said Ms. Sewall. "But a good filmmaker is a lot like a detective. She's got to have a sharp eye for detail, to see what others don't see. And she's got to be good at putting together pieces, to make a complete picture.

"We'll be doing two important things at your new media center. One, you'll be making videos, and two, I'll be restoring a clip from an old black film made in 1932, *The Talk of the Town*. Your videos and my old film will premiere at a gala opening at the media center. Press, parents, everyone will be invited."

"Hey!" "Wow!" "Cool!" Everybody in class was so excited, they all started talking at the same time.

"My uncle Buddy was in the movies . . . a movie," I shouted.

19

"Yeah," said Alphonso, "*Nightmare on Elm Street*, part sixty." Everyone laughed.

"No," I said. "A long, *long* time ago, when you couldn't hear people talk in the movies. You could only hear pianos or organs. And I was named after a movie star, Ella DuChamps!"

Ms. Sewall gave me a funny look, as if the name meant something to her. "Ella DuChamps?"

Just then Mrs. Henderson took over. "All right, class, enough questions—and Ella, enough of your life story. I suggest you all gather your books and go over your homework assignments. Make use of your time before the bell rings."

I was so excited, I followed Ms. Sewall over to Mrs. Henderson's desk, but they began to talk, so I couldn't interrupt.

I overheard Ms. Sewall say, "That was very odd. How would that child know the name Ella DuChamps? She was a famous black starlet in the 1930s. Only a real film buff or historian would know her name."

I was about to tell Ms. Sewall, but the bell rang. The class was on its feet and heading for the door. I was swept along by the crowd.

"Remember," shouted Ms. Sewall, "you're my video

cadets! Keep your eyes peeled and your lens in focus!"

I couldn't wait till I saw her again. And boy, wait till Uncle Buddy finds out I'm making a movie! Who would believe that all I could worry about this morning was Alphonso Green beating me to a pulp, and now I was going to make a movie! What a day!

SCENE 3

Action: *What the director yells to tell the actors to begin moving and speaking. Action is also used to describe everything that's happening on the screen.*

"Don't you look fancy," remarked Mr. Simms. "Looks like you're about to yell 'Action!'"

"Uncle Buddy! Uncle Buddy, I've got so much to tell you!" I yelled, running up to him. He was sweeping the sidewalk outside Jackson's Barbershop on Columbia Road.

"Not now, honey. I'll be there in a minute," he said as he continued to sweep, complaining about the empty cups and sandwich wrappers from Lorenzo's.

I walked into the empty barbershop, took a deep breath of my favorite smell, and read my favorite word on the bottle of blue liquid that held eight combs—each a different size, each meant for doing different things with hair.

"Antiseptic, antiseptic, antiseptic." The word rolled

22

over my tongue like a marble rolling around a pinball game.

For a long time I had thought the word *antiseptic* meant the sharp, sweet smells of the barbershop. Uncle Buddy's smell, too. Then one Sunday morning on our way out the door to go to church, I cheerfully told Mom that she sure smelled antiseptic. She gave me a funny look and explained that *antiseptic* meant very, very clean and that something antiseptic usually didn't smell at all, but she would take it as a compliment anyway. Oh, well. It was still one of my favorite words. *Antiseptic, antiseptic, antiseptic.*

Since my dad didn't get home until 4:30, and Mom's arrival depended on her shift at the hospital, I sometimes had to go to Uncle Buddy's barbershop after school. I did my homework or helped with chores, like folding clean towels still warm from the dryer, or putting the caps back on bottles of spicy-smelling hair tonic.

Sometimes I would just sit in one of the barber chairs and spin slowly, listening to the stories told by Uncle Buddy and the barbershop regulars, Mr. Perry, Mr. McKnight, and Mr. Simms.

I got a soda out of the small refrigerator in the back, bypassing the milk Mom made sure was there for me. Milk. Yuck. Mr. Perry, Mr. Simms, and Mr. McKnight

23

helped me out by using it in their coffee. They drank a lot of coffee. I couldn't decide which they did most—drink coffee or talk.

I wondered where they were. I had so much to tell them. This had been my best day at school in a long time. There were a hundred ideas in my head, ideas that would make great movies.

And no matter how hard Alphonso tried to get me in trouble, I would ignore him and concentrate on my movie. Now that I was going to be a director, I had bigger fish to fry than Alphonso Green.

Uncle Buddy was still outside sweeping, so I opened up my books. Nothing left to do but start my homework. Then I heard laughter and voices. The barbershop regulars! Good, wait till they hear I'm going to make a movie! I went to the barbershop window to look for them.

Hot pinpricks filled my cheeks. Alphonso! Talking to *my* guys. Uncle Buddy cut Alphonso's hair twice a month. Sometimes he would hang out at the barbershop, but not on my days. It was sort of an unspoken rule.

"Hey, Ella," said Alphonso. He spun his basketball on a finger. "I was just telling Mr. Simms, Mr. Perry, and Mr. McKnight about the basketball league semifinals."

"I bet you didn't tell them about our one-on-one yesterday when I stomped you into the ground, did you?" I said, sticking my tongue out and wiggling my fingers. I knew I was asking for trouble.

"I *let* you win at keep-away because I felt sorry for you. Next time, I won't let you off so easy, nerd."

"I won fair and square because I'm a better player, so deal with that."

Alphonso bounced his basketball hard on the ground.

"Ella, even if you did win—," said Uncle Buddy.

"If?"

"Who won is not the point. You're both fine players, and I'll be at the Boys' Club to see Alphonso play in the semifinals. After all, your dad's coaching."

Mr. Simms, Mr. Perry, and Mr. McKnight agreed in unison.

"See you around, Ella!" Alphonso grinned smugly as he bounced his ball down the street.

I slowly followed Uncle Buddy into the barbershop and sat in my corner. Mr. Perry picked up his copy of the *Washington Afro-American,* but instead of reading it, he looked at me and asked, "Are you all right? You're awful quiet."

"I'm okay."

Uncle Buddy dusted off the seat of one of the barber

chairs and waved me over to sit in it. I climbed into the chair and Uncle Buddy stepped on the bar at the bottom to make it rise. Usually this made me giggle, but not today.

"So you beat Alphonso at one-on-one?" Uncle Buddy questioned.

"Yeah. In front of the Posse. I'm dead meat."

"You and Alphonso ought to stop that bickering," said Mr. McKnight.

"But it's not me," I cried. "He won't leave me alone."

Uncle Buddy chuckled. "Sounds like puppy love to me."

"That's disgusting!" I jumped out of the barber chair and went to a corner where there was a pile of freshly dried towels. I began folding them.

"When are you two going to be friends again?" Uncle Buddy asked.

"Never in a million, *bazillion* years."

"Don't talk like that," my uncle scolded.

"He stole my dollar and he called me a liar, right in front of the whole class."

"Why'd he call you a liar?"

"He called your stories *lies*, Uncle Buddy," I said to him in a have-you-ever-heard-anything-more-terrible tone of voice.

"Lies!" said Mr. Perry. "Why, child, that's no insult where we come from. We used to call all the tall tales lies. Down home, we had lying contests on many a Saturday night at the Elm Street General Store. And the one with the biggest, most bodacious tale would take home a smoked ham!"

"Ham?" said Mr. McKnight. "Smoked ham?"

"Biggest, sweetest, pinkest you've ever seen."

"Naw, man, not the sweetest . . ."

And that's how their stories always began. One word would set them off, and soon somebody would be telling a story about one bigger, sweeter, and prettier, and how it came to be that way.

Just then the door swung open. A man holding a clipboard entered, rolling a large trunk tied to a dolly. "I have a delivery for a Mr. W. B. Jackson."

"I'm W. B. Jackson," said Uncle Buddy. "What's this?"

"Don't know, but it came all the way from Canada."

I went over to look at the trunk and, sure enough, there was a sticker of the Canadian flag. We had just finished studying flags of the world, and I recognized the red maple leaf right away.

"What is it, Uncle Buddy?" I asked. I didn't understand why Uncle Buddy didn't look excited. I knew I would be,

27

if someone delivered a huge trunk from Canada for me. Didn't he want to know what was inside?

Uncle Buddy picked up the envelope taped to the top of the trunk and opened it. Inside was a letter on light pink paper.

He read the letter silently, and from the expression on his face, I thought they must have been the saddest words in the world. Mr. McKnight, Mr. Simms, and Mr. Perry gave one another puzzled glances. They didn't know what was going on, either.

I moved closer to Uncle Buddy, waiting and hoping he would explain why he was so sad. Was something bad in the trunk?

When Uncle Buddy finished reading the letter, he folded it up neatly and put it in his back pocket. Then, as if the trunk were not even there, he went back to folding towels.

"Aren't you going to open it, Uncle Buddy?" I asked. I ran my fingers across the top, feeling the rough cord that held the trunk closed.

"Hush, Ella," Mr. Simms said. "I think it's personal."

"Is it personal, Uncle Buddy?"

Uncle Buddy put down the towel he was folding and went back to the trunk. He pulled away the cords and stood a moment, just staring at it.

28

Without realizing it, we all leaned forward.

He opened the trunk.

Old, yellow, balled-up newspapers sat on top, protecting whatever was inside.

"Give me a hand," he said to me.

I excitedly tossed the little balls of newspaper from the trunk. It seemed as if there was nothing but newspaper until . . .

"WOW!"

I planted my feet and lifted up a heavy round movie canister.

"Movies!" I squealed with delight. My eyes grew bigger as I looked down. "And more movies! Big ones, little ones, movies, movies, movies!"

"Oh, my stars!" muttered Mr. Perry at the sight. We all stood, gazing down into the trunk.

"There must be a hundred at least!" said a startled Mr. McKnight.

"Only fifty or so," said Uncle Buddy. He didn't sound any happier now that the box was open. As a matter of fact, he sounded a lot sadder.

I picked up a rusty film can and blew dust away from the label.

"Hey! *The Lonesome Trail*? I know this story!" I said

29

excitedly. "You told me this story. You never told me it was a movie. I thought you made it up!"

"I did," said Uncle Buddy. "I wrote it a long time ago."

"And made it into a movie?"

"Yes."

"Are all of these your movies?"

"I guess you could say that."

Mr. Simms, Mr. McKnight, and Mr. Perry helped me pull film cans and reels from the box, reading each label. I knew every title, because Uncle Buddy had told me each and every one of those stories.

"Stories, our stories are really movies! Uncle Buddy, this is incredible!" I said. "Why didn't you ever tell me you made movies?"

Uncle Buddy reached into the box and pulled out a bent envelope and a battered red hat.

"That must have been a nice fedora in its day. I'm sure somebody cut a sharp figure in it," said Mr. Simms.

"She did," said Uncle Buddy. He gently touched the scraggly feather sticking out of the hat. From the envelope Uncle Buddy pulled out an old faded photograph of a dark, handsome man wearing jodhpurs—those funny pants people who ride horses wear—and a beautiful woman wearing a fedora.

30

I stared at the picture and suddenly recognized the fedora and the man.

"Uncle Buddy, that's you! And the lady's wearing this hat!"

"Don't you look fancy," remarked Mr. Simms. "Looks like you're about to yell 'Action!'"

"Yep. I was very young then. Thought I was on my way to becoming a successful moviemaker. Every film in that box is one I worked on. I wrote them, I directed them. I was even in one or two of them."

"Just like Spike Lee," I said, awestruck.

"Who's the lady in the picture?" Mr. Perry asked.

"That is Ella DuChamps."

"Ella DuChamps? *My* Ella DuChamps? The woman you named me after? Was she your girlfriend?"

"If you mean, did I love her? Yes. Very much. And she was one of the most talented actresses I ever had the pleasure of working with. She was one of a kind."

"Where is she now?"

"Well, that's why the letter made me so sad, Ella. Ella DuChamps has passed away. She had been holding on to these old films for a long time now, and I guess she thought I'd like to have them when she was gone."

I reached over and hugged my great uncle.

31

"Thank you, Ella," Uncle Buddy said. He got up and firmly closed the trunk.

"Come on, McKnight," he said. "Thelma wants you home for dinner on time for a change. Let's get you taken care of. A little off the sides?" Mr. McKnight got into the barber chair, and Uncle Buddy wrapped a blue drape around him and thin tissue paper around his neck.

"But Uncle Buddy, you're a movie director!" I said, almost yelling.

"No, baby, I'm a barber," he said firmly. He turned on the electric clippers.

"Uncle Buddy, you're not going to throw these away, are you?"

"To tell you the truth, Ella, I don't know what I'm going to do with them."

"Can we look at them?"

"I don't think so. We'll just find a place to put this trunk and leave it there."

"Uncle Buddy, if you don't want these movies, can I have them?"

"What for? What do you want to do with these old things?"

"Well," I began, "I can take them to school with me and show everybody that I'm not a liar, and that you

32

did make movies and we can watch them and—"

Uncle Buddy stood up, looking angry. "No." He stopped cutting Mr. McKnight's hair and pushed the trunk toward the back room. "They're staying right here. They're no good to anybody. Not to you, not to me."

"But they're *movies*!" I cried, following Uncle Buddy. "Real movies. Not just stories you told me and I told friends! *Wild Bill Pickett, The Lonesome Trail*—"

"I said *no*!"

There was a surprised silence in the barbershop. Uncle Buddy had never raised his voice to me before. Tears came to my eyes. Why was he so sad and angry when he should feel proud of all the movies in the trunk? This had to be one of those grown-up things I could never understand.

My stories were movies! Movies! I hadn't even had a chance to tell Uncle Buddy about Ms. Sewall and my movie, first because of Alphonso's showing up at the barbershop on my day, and then because of the trunk's arrival.

Alphonso was mad at me for something that wasn't my fault, and now Uncle Buddy, who should be jumping for joy at getting his movies back, was so angry about it that he yelled at me. How did things get so crazy?

33

SCENE 4

Frame: *A strip of film is made up of several single pictures. Each picture is called a* frame. *It takes twenty-four frames moving through the projector to create one second of movement on the screen.*

"Movies are only still pictures—photographs—called frames, *shown very quickly, one after another, so you just* think *you're seeing motion."*

Usually I hate Mondays, but after a weekend of silence from Uncle Buddy—and my parents, who told me not even to mention the word "movie" because it upset him so—I was glad to be back in the noisy halls of Bancroft. Uncle Buddy, who always had a smile for me or a story to tell, had been very quiet on Saturday in the barbershop. On Sunday, he had barely left his room except to eat. What had I done wrong?

As I walked onto the playground, I noticed that Juanita had put her videocassette pin on her coat! Ms. Sewall! I had forgotten that Ms. Sewall would be teaching us three mornings a week until the end of the semester.

34

"Good morning, Ella," Ms. Sewall said to me as I took off my heavy backpack. Hey! She remembered me!

When the class was settled, two sixth graders on the audiovisual squad came in, pushing a big television set and VCR on a rolling cart. Ms. Sewall put a tape into the VCR and said, "Today, ladies and gentlemen, we are going to have our first lesson in filmmaking. You have to learn to watch a movie differently from the way most people do. Soon watching TV and movies will be a completely different experience for you.

"Movies are only still pictures—photographs—called *frames*, shown very quickly, one after another, so you just *think* you're seeing motion. That's why when movies were first invented, they were called *moving pictures*, which was later shortened into the word *movies*."

Ms. Sewall picked up a stack of faded black-and-white pictures and spread them out for us to see. They all had the same picture on them, except that in the last one, the lady had her hat on instead of in her hand. Then Ms. Sewall put them all back together and quickly flipped them like a stack of cards. It was really great because as Ms. Sewall flipped, it looked like the lady in the picture actually put on her hat!

"What's this?" she said, holding up a black-and-white

35

marble composition book.

Confused, the class mumbled, "A notebook."

"That's correct, but what kind of notebook? What does this word mean?" she asked, pointing to the front.

"*Composition* means something written—a paragraph, a story. What's writing got to do with the movies?" asked Renee.

"Good question, Renee," Ms. Sewall responded. "When you write a story or paragraph, you put the idea together in a certain way so your reader will pay attention to the right thing at the right moment. Would you all be interested in 'The Three Little Pigs' if I started the story with the wolf falling down the chimney into a big black pot of boiling water?"

"I would!" said Alphonso. The entire class giggled. Even I had to laugh.

"Very funny, Alphonso," Ms. Sewall said with a smile. "Now you're going to help me teach you how a director uses composition. Composition in filmmaking means that each picture you see on the screen tells you what to look at, what is most important in the story."

"But if the picture keeps moving, how do you figure out what's important?" I asked.

"You look at the way the director designs the shot.

Objects or people are placed in certain ways. Things look bigger or smaller, depending on how critical they are to the scene."

The rest of the morning was wild and fun. Ms. Sewall divided us into groups: background, foreground, and middle ground, the three parts of every picture. A fourth group stood at the back of the room, as the audience. Ms. Sewall arranged us in different poses on different levels, standing on chairs and desks, sitting on the floor. She would even tell us to change our expressions from happy to sad to blank.

Then she'd yell, "Freeze" (which we were really good at, except for a few giggles and twitches here and there). The audience at the back of the room had to decide who they thought was important in the picture, and Ms. Sewall would explain why the eye was drawn to that person. What a great class!

At the end of class she gave each of us a packet of actual photographs—stills—from recent movies. For homework we were to decide which part of the pictures the director was trying to get us to look at—the background, foreground, or middle ground—and match the picture with the shot.

*   *   *

My mom was working the evening shift at the hospital, so

37

she was home when I finished school that day. She watched me clear off the dining room table and set out my photos.

"Okay, Mom, this is how it goes. There's background, foreground, and middle ground," I explained.

"What happened to addition, subtraction, and long division?" she asked.

"Chill, Mom," I said. "This is the media generation."

"Oh dear," she said, sounding worried.

Half an hour later, we were both saying, "Oh dear." What had seemed so clear with Manuel and Renee standing on the desk and Debra and Alphonso on the floor now seemed confusing. My carefully printed labels with the words *background*, *foreground*, and *middle ground* lay in a heap. The pictures scattered around the table refused to arrange themselves in any kind of order.

The phone rang, and Mom gratefully went to answer it. I rested my head on my arms, wishing for a distraction of my own.

Uncle Buddy came through the dining room on his way to the kitchen for a cup of coffee. I gave him a weak high five, along with a sigh.

"You'll never guess who that was, Uncle Buddy," Mom said as she got off the phone.

Uncle Buddy returned from the kitchen, coffee cup in

hand, and the two of them talked about an old family friend.

As they talked, Uncle Buddy began moving my pictures around absentmindedly.

"Look at the time. I'd better get dinner started," Mom said.

"But Mom, what about my homework?"

"Maybe after dinner, sweetie."

"Can Uncle Buddy help—"

Mom silently mouthed the word "No!"

Uncle Buddy took another sip of coffee, still playing with the pictures on the table. "You know, Ella," he said, "people are really so interesting."

"*Umph*," I grunted, thinking he was talking about the family friend who had just called. I continued to stare at my homework assignment. People *are* interesting, I thought, suddenly noticing that the first thing you looked at in each picture were the *people*. Sure enough, they were all in the foreground in the row Uncle Buddy had arranged.

"Background, background, background," I said, putting together the next row. Now I understood! I turned around to yell "Thanks!" but he had already left the room.

*　　*　　*

Wednesday's class was great. Ms. Sewall taped my home-work to the board and referred to it throughout the period.

At the end of class she announced, "On Friday, we'll pass out Polaroid cameras, and we'll go on a little field trip. You'll be taking pictures of whatever you find inter-esting, keeping composition in mind. Remember, with every picture you compose, you're telling me what to look at. On our trip you can take pictures of cars, or birds, or people walking by, anything. You'll be working in teams of two, so I'll assign partners."

I waited to hear my name called. I glanced across the room and saw Alphonso whispering to Akil. I knew he was still plotting revenge. He made a face at me, and I made one right back. This kept up until Alphonso threw a pencil at me. I gave him a mean look and turned my back to him. "Alphonso Green and Ella Jackson," said Ms. Sewall.

"No!" I cried.

"No way," said Alphonso.

"You're partners."

"But Ms. Sewall—"

"No complaints, please."

Alphonso and I looked at each other. Of all the bad luck! I knew we were both thinking the same thing. If we

40

made up enough to actually work together as partners, the whole class would start teasing us again about being boyfriend and girlfriend. But if we continued to fight, we'd get a U on our project.

I rested my head on my desk. Could life get any worse?

I managed to make it through the rest of the day without making Mrs. Henderson angry and without thinking too much about Alphonso and our—yuck—partnership. After math, spelling, language arts, and phys ed, school was finally over.

My route from the gym took me past the media center. I noticed Ms. Sewall was there. She smiled when she saw me and motioned me in.

"You did really well in class today, Ella. How do you know so much about filmmaking?"

"My Uncle Buddy helped me with my homework, and we go to the movies all the time."

"That sounds like fun. Are you thinking about a career as a filmmaker when you grow up?"

"I'm thinking about it. Oh, Ms. Sewall, speaking of careers, today we got our handouts for the Career Day assembly next week. Why don't you speak at the assembly? Then all the kids, not just the kids you're teaching, can find out what you do."

"That's a great idea, Ella. Is anyone coming from your family?"

"I don't know yet . . . maybe my mom, maybe my dad . . . and . . . maybe . . . maybe . . ."

"Ella? What is it? You look like the cat that just swallowed the canary!"

"Maybe my great-uncle Buddy!" I said excitedly. What a great idea! If Uncle Buddy came for Career Day, Ms. Sewall could help him understand that he should be proud of his movies. Now all I had to do was come up with a plan to convince Uncle Buddy. No problem!

SCENE 5

Bird's-Eye View: *The scene is shot from above, as if you are looking down on the action. It's how a bird would see things happening on the ground if it was flying in the sky or sitting in a tree.*

I found myself in the hall with a bird's-eye view of my mother at the bottom of the steps. And she looked just about as annoyed as I felt.

We all loved it when Mom worked the night shift. It meant everyone had time to eat dinner together before she went to work. As a special treat, she always made a great dessert. Tonight she'd made apple cobbler!

Now, when to put the plan into action? Before dessert or after?

"Here you are, Uncle Buddy," Mom said, smiling. She served him a large helping of cobbler topped with a scoop of vanilla ice cream. "This will cure whatever ails you!"

"Nothing ailing me, but if there was, this would make it skedaddle."

"We're having Career Day next week," I announced—casually, I hoped.

"It's not my turn," said Dad. "I went last year, and there were two other parents who were computer programmers. I didn't get a word in!"

"When is it, Ella?" Mom asked. "Maybe they'll be interested in a nurse. I think I'm working evenings next week, so I can probably do it."

"Well . . . actually I was hoping maybe Uncle Buddy could come this year, to talk about movies."

Forks were put down. Throats were cleared.

"So what did I say?" I asked.

"Ella, I don't think that's such a good idea," Mom said slowly.

"Now, now, Brenda," said my dad. "Let her ask once and get an answer. Then we won't hear anything more about this, will we, Ella?"

"Uncle Buddy, will you please, please, please come to my class to talk about movies?"

"Nope," answered Uncle Buddy, not missing a beat.

"There, Ella, you've got your answer. The subject is closed," said Dad.

44

"That's right, closed," Mom added. Still, I knew from my mother's voice that it wasn't *completely* closed.

"But you know, Uncle Buddy," Mom continued as she got up to clear the dessert dishes, "there's something special about making movies. The glamour, the history."

"No glamour," said Uncle Buddy, "just hard work and hard times. May I have some coffee, please?" Mom went to the kitchen to get his coffee.

"But it must have been fun, Uncle Buddy!" I said.

"Don't worry him, Ella," said Dad.

"Those films are a bunch of forgettable two-reelers that most people would laugh at today. They're not history, they're a part of my life that I don't want dug up. Excuse me."

Uncle Buddy left the table, passing Mom as she returned with his coffee.

I excused myself and went upstairs to do my homework.

Later I heard music coming from Uncle Buddy's room. It was Billie Holiday. Uncle Buddy told me she sang in the 1940s, and the record was so old you could hear scratchy, popping sounds. Yet even with all the scratchy noise, the voice singing the words, "Lately I find, you're on my mind, more than you know," was incredibly sad and beautiful.

45

Uncle Buddy listened to Billie Holiday only when he was feeling low about something.

I peeked in his door. He was singing softly with the record, holding the fedora from the trunk. He looked up and caught me peering at him through the crack in the door.

"You're like a bad penny. Always turning up when I least expect it."

I pushed the door open, but hung back at the entrance.

"You sad tonight?"

"Not sad, just thinking."

I sat on the edge of the bed, tracing my finger around the nubby pattern on the bedspread.

"Ms. Sewall liked my homework you helped me with. I want to tell her about your movies but she may not believe me, unless . . . You know how it is when grown-ups give you that fake smile and say, 'That's nice, dear.' And Alphonso will make it worse. He'll say I'm lying about the movies, because he always thinks I'm lying."

"And if you could just show them the movies—"

"Right!" I exclaimed.

"No way, José."

I stretched across the bed and picked up an old family photo from Uncle Buddy's nightstand.

46

"But you told me about all the other things that happened to you. Like when you were a bricklayer, and working in the factories in the discretion—"

"Depression."

"Depression. And when you delivered your sister Sukie because the midwife was late. Why can't you tell me about when you made movies?"

Uncle Buddy took the photo and put it back on the nightstand.

"This is not show-and-tell. This is my private life."

"But what about *my* life? Ms. Sewall is teaching us how to make movies. Maybe I could be a director like you."

"You can't, you're a girl."

"Yes I can," I said, surprised he'd say such a thing.

"No, you can't," said Uncle Buddy.

That made me mad. "I can be anything I want to be, and being a girl doesn't have anything to do with it," I told him.

"Ella! Ella!" Mom's voice floated up the stairs, running down the list of my bedtime routine.

"You better go," sighed Uncle Buddy. As I reached the door he said, "You're lucky."

"Why do you say that?"

"You can stand here now and say that you can be

47

anything you want to be, and it's almost true. Once I thought *I* could be anything I wanted to be—but then I found out different."

"Who, what, where, when? What are you talking about? Making movies?"

"Ella!" My mother's voice sounded angrier.

"Even if you weren't a girl, you wouldn't want to make movies. It's a hard, hard life."

"Ella!" I knew Mom was on her way up. Uncle Buddy gave me a push out the door. I found myself in the hall with a bird's-eye view of my mother at the bottom of the steps. And she looked just about as annoyed as I felt.

SCENE 6

Another Angle: *You see the same picture, but from a different position.*

I swung myself upside down on the monkey bars and dangled there for a minute before I realized that I was looking at Ms. Sewall from another angle.

Career Day was sort of interesting, and Mom was the only nurse this year. Ms. Sewall did come to the assembly, but since my plan had failed big-time, instead of chatting with Uncle Buddy about movies, she chatted with Mom about nursing. The next day was just plain dull—no parents, no assemblies, no excitement at all. Was I glad to see Friday and Ms. Sewall in her white lab jacket.

The lab seemed to have more machines, test tubes, and books every time I came. Every object, large or small, was interesting. "Ella, put that down," had come from Ms. Sewall's lips several times before we even started class. Ms. Sewall pulled on her safety goggles and picked up a large pair of tweezers.

49

"All right, gather round, class." We bunched up around the lab table and watched as she picked up a long strip of film.

"This is the heart and soul of film preservation. Nitrate film stock. It has to be handled with great care—it can be very dangerous."

"Why is it dangerous, Ms. Sewall?" I asked.

"I'll show you. Everybody take two steps back." She pulled a cigarette lighter from her pocket, flicked it once, and touched it to the tip of the film strip. Within a second the film was a long strip of glowing, yellow flame.

Every kid took a third step back and shared one long gasp of surprise. Ms. Sewall quickly dropped it into a round glass dish, where it became a small heap of ashes.

"*Peeee-yewwww!*" we all shouted, holding our noses.

"Not the most pleasant smell, is it? As you can see and smell, nitrates react violently when they come in contact with heat and chemicals. Lesson one: Be very, very careful with nitrate stock. Benny, lights, please, and let's go on to our next lesson in film preservation."

Ms. Sewall turned on the VCR, and we rearranged ourselves so we could see. Large black-and-white numbers flashed on the screen. This, Ms. Sewall explained, was the leader, a length of film put on at the beginning to allow the

50

projectionist time for any last-minute focusing before the actual film started.

The scratched, silent picture of a handsome black man in a dashing white cowboy hat appeared on the TV screen.

"The films of the past were all shot on nitrate stock. Very little survived. I've been working on getting what's left of this one into good condition so it can be shown at the gala. Small pieces of films like this one, *Fire on the Wind*, with Whitney Lloyd, are pretty much all we have left. Mr. Lloyd was considered one of the first black matinee idols."

"His hair looks funny," said Alphonso. Whitney Lloyd's hair was really straight and slicked back.

"That's called a *process*." Ms. Sewall laughed. "It was pretty popular back then. Now pay attention to this," she said, pointing to the screen. "That's an interesting angle, don't you think?"

"It's spooky," I said.

"Very spooky. The director could have chosen a different angle, and it wouldn't have been spooky at all. It may have been funny or sad. The director chose to shoot it this way because he wanted to communicate to us that the hero, Whitney Lloyd, was in trouble.

"Your assignment today is to take pictures of objects

51

around the school, keeping in mind what feeling you want to express. If you want spooky or funny or sad, think about where you are, where the object is, and where you want to put the camera. Same partners as before."

Bam! Alphonso slammed a book down on his desk. Everyone turned toward him. He mumbled "Sorry" and slowly joined me in line for cameras and film.

We sat on the swings, the camera on the ground between us. The other kids raced around taking pictures, laughing and having a great time. Alphonso dug his toe into the hollow in the dirt scooped out by every kid that had ever been on that swing.

"So," he said.

"So what," I said.

"So you gonna take any pictures, Ms. Smarty-pants?"

"Why don't you take some, Mr. Know-it-all?"

"Why should I?" he asked, getting off the swing. "If I'm nice and help Ms. Sewall with stuff, she'll give me a C anyway. What's the point of fooling with all this stupid camera stuff, anyway?"

He hated movies. He hated me. And I hated him right back.

A basketball lay in the corner of the playground. Alphonso went and got it and came back across, dribbling with a behind-the-back move so smooth that all I could think was, Wow. I had been working on that all summer. I looked up, squinting into the sun, and saw the building and Ms. Sewall standing in the second-floor lab.

I swung myself upside down on the monkey bars and dangled there for a minute before I realized that I was looking at Ms. Sewall from another angle. She was holding up a strip of film to get a better view of it.

Wow! A great idea appeared in my head, just like those cartoons of a lightbulb turning on.

I jumped down and headed for the building. As I ran past Alphonso, I shouted for him to bring the camera.

When we arrived at the media center, Ms. Sewall was gone.

"Where'd she go that fast?" I wondered.

"Beats me. So why are we here?"

"Suppose we get Ms. Sewall to burn a piece of film for us and we shoot her from down low, looking up. Pretty scary, huh? Just like a mad scientist?"

"Yeah," agreed Alphonso enthusiastically, to my surprise. "But she's not here, so how can we do it? We only have ten minutes before the bell rings."

"We'll get everything ready." I turned to the nearby supply shelf to get the tweezers and a tray. I had to stand

53

on my toes and stretch to reach the top shelf. I made a long reach for the tweezers. As I grabbed them, my hand hit a brown bottle with the word ACETONE printed on it in large capital letters. It fell and broke, spilling into the opened film can.

I was paralyzed. My eyes got as big as doorknobs as I heard the sizzle. Little rivers of smoke began to rise from the opened film can, the acetone still going *glug, glug, glug,* onto the curled-up film.

Ms. Sewall opened the door and screamed. She ran from one end of the lab table to the next, squealing as the piece of film quickly dissolved in the acetone.

"My film, oh no! Oh no!"

"I'm sorry, Ms. Sewall! I didn't mean—"

"Sorry? This is five years of my life! Raising money, searching for the missing pieces . . . Look at this, it's ruined!"

Ms. Sewall kept running back and forth, sort of like a tennis ball going over and over the net. As she ran, our heads followed her, turning from left to right and left again. The whole thing would have been funny if it wasn't so horrible.

I was speechless. The words "I'm sorry" weren't going to be enough, and the tears welling up in my eyes weren't going to help, either, but I couldn't stop them. The late-bell rang.

"You two get to class," she said, finally stopping, out of breath, and leaning on the lab table.

She was letting us leave! The brick sitting on my chest suddenly got lighter.

"You mean you're not sending me to the office?"

Alphonso had my elbow and was pulling me toward the door, muttering under his breath, "Don't ask questions, let's just get out of here."

"No," said Ms. Sewall. "It wouldn't bring the film back."

"You heard her, let's go!" Alphonso gave one last pull and I was through the door.

"Oh boy, oh boy, oh boy!" I said, shaking my head as we walked down the hall.

"You and your stupid ideas!" Alphonso said through gritted teeth.

"Well, it sure beats being just plain stupid!" I fired back.

"Take it back!"

"Will not!"

He punched me on the shoulder. It hurt. I hit him back. The licks started flying, and soon we were fighting in earnest.

"That's enough!" Ms. Sewall's voice rang out with such

55

cold anger that we both stopped in midblow and turned to look at her. Her arms were folded across her chest, and her eyes were filled with disgust.

"You have crossed the line. OUT NOW!" She turned on her heel and went back into the classroom.

Alphonso and I let go of each other. I broke into tears, crying with such long, loud sobs that I couldn't catch my breath.

"Oh, man! Stop that! Don't cry! See, that's what's wrong with you now, you're such a . . . girl!"

"I'm not a girl!" I yelled back, knowing that he meant it in the worst possible way. Giggling. Silly. Weak.

I knew there was nothing wrong with liking girl things. But those weren't the only things I liked.

And Alphonso knew that—after all, I'd beaten him at basketball.

"When did you get to be such a boy! Not a boy, a bully!"

He knew what I meant. The strut, having to win, picking on someone in a way that went far beyond a little teasing.

"We used to be friends," I said.

"A friend wouldn't have beat me in front of the Posse."

"A friend would have known that I had been in a

56

summer basketball camp at Georgetown University."

Alphonso's mouth dropped open.

"You're kidding!"

"No. Patrick Ewing was a guest one day, and John Thompson was in and out all the time."

"You didn't tell me!"

"You didn't ask."

We didn't know what to say after that. Was there any chance we could be friends again after all this time?

I stuck my hand up for Alphonso to give me a high five. I stood there, hand in the air, not looking in his direction, trying not to be scared that he would leave me hanging. Trying not to be scared that maybe it was too late to be friends.

My palm tingled as his hand hit mine.

"Go wash your face," he said.

I went into the girls' bathroom for a towel to wipe my face. By the time I came out, my face was still tear-stained, but my eyes were bright.

"Alphonso! I've got an idea!"

"Luuuuuuucy!" he said, just like Ricky Ricardo on the *I Love Lucy* show. "You know you only get into trouble when you start thinking up these crazy ideas," he continued in a Cuban accent.

It worked. I couldn't help laughing. Alphonso could be okay when he wanted to be.

"No, really, I can fix it. Come on."

We went back to the room. Ms. Sewall was still sitting where we had left her, staring at the black smoky mess on the countertop.

"Ms. Sewall, I know you hate me right now, but—"

"Don't be silly, Ella. I'm mad at you, and I'm upset about the film you ruined, but I don't hate you."

"If you'll only please, please listen, I think I can make it better."

"I doubt it, Ella. Mrs. Henderson was right about you. You are a handful."

"She's not right!" I spoke quickly so I could get my idea out before she kicked us out again. "If you give me a chance, I can prove it. It's about my uncle Buddy. A trunk full of his old movies came to the barbershop the other day, and if I can get you one of his movies to replace the one we just ruined—"

"Movies? A trunk full of movies?" she said softly, with just enough of a question in her voice to tell me that I had her interest.

"No, no," Ms. Sewall said, shaking her head. "I'm so upset, I'm grasping at straws. Ella, stop letting your imagi-

58

nation run away with you. Your uncle Buddy, who I'm sure is a very nice man, probably has old family movies."

"No! These are real movies, the kind people used to go to in theaters. *Lonesome Trail, Manhattan at Midnight*—"

"Those are classics. How do you know those titles?" she asked, suddenly paying close attention.

"My uncle Buddy told them to me as bedtime stories, but he didn't tell me they were movies until I saw them myself in this trunk."

"It's true, Ms. Sewall. I've seen the trunk myself, but he won't let anybody touch it," added Alphonso.

"Maybe he just saw them when he was young," Ms. Sewall said slowly, still not willing to believe.

"No! He wrote them! His name is on the film cans."

"What is your uncle's name?"

"Uncle Buddy."

"No, his real name, stupid," said Alphonso.

"Oh. Buddy Jackson."

"Buddy . . . Buddy Jackson? Is Buddy a nickname?" Ms. Sewall asked, drumming her fingers on the desk.

"Yeah, his real name is William, I think, but we never call him that."

"William Jackson . . . W. B. Jackson! Oh my God! He and his films disappeared in the early thirties! He was a

59

legend. Ella, if you're right, we could both be saved. Tell me about the films. What kind of shape are they in?"

Ms. Sewall was really excited, and I forget about all the trouble I'd been in just a few minutes ago.

"They're kind of dusty. Some of them have this brown gunk on them."

"Of course," Ms. Sewall muttered to herself, "nitrate deterioration. How many reels, do you know what gauge?"

"Reels? Oh, you mean cans. I didn't count. Uncle Buddy wouldn't let me. What's a gauge?"

"Never mind," she said, impatient for all the details. "When can I talk to him?"

"Um . . . I don't know. I'm not even sure I should have told you about them."

"But of course you should have," Ms. Sewall said with a puzzled frown.

"You don't know her uncle Buddy," said Alphonso.

"I'm supposed to respect his privacy," said Ella.

"But why would he want to keep something so wonderful private? When can I see one? Just let me talk to him."

"I can't, Ms. Sewall. He feels very funny about them. I'll talk to him. I'll try and see if I can change his mind."

"Ella, you're a peach! Just think, I'm going to see films by W. B. Jackson!"

Alphonso gave me a look, and we both backed out of the room. It was nice to see Ms. Sewall smiling again, but . . .

"Are you crazy? How do you think you're going to get your uncle Buddy to give up his movies?"

"I don't know," was the only thing I could say. Now I understood that funny old saying of Uncle Buddy's—"Caught between a rock and a hard place."

SCENE 7

Dailies: *Each day after shooting, the director and crew look at the film footage shot that day. They call this footage dailies.*

I lay in bed that night, replaying in my mind what had happened in the barbershop that day, just like a director looking at dailies.

I had a mission. I had to help Uncle Buddy understand that his movies were important and should be shared with the world. But I didn't have the slightest idea of how to accomplish it.

So I called Alphonso and asked him to come over right away. I told him there was a big piece of Boston cream pie waiting for him.

Asphonso ate two pieces to my one and went straight to my backyard to shoot some hoops.

"The idea is to get it *into* the basket, Alphonso," I said, standing at the back door as I ate my last bite of pie.

"Yeah, right," he said sarcastically.

"Look, if your uncle said no to giving you the movies and no to Career Day, and your parents have told you not to talk to him about it, I don't see how his movies are going to get you out of trouble," said Alphonso. "Face it. Ms. Sewall is going to flunk you, tell the principal that you ruined her film, the media center will be closed down, and you'll get kicked out of school." The ball bounced off the backboard for the third time.

"I'll get kicked out of school?" I jumped down the steps and stole the ball from Alphonso in one smooth move. Try *we'll* get kicked out of school. You were there—you'll get kicked out, too!"

"Will not."

"Will too, we're partners, remember?"

"It wasn't my idea to firebomb her movie."

"Your fingerprints were on everything, too."

"That's it," Alphonso said, tucking the basketball under his arm. "I'm outta here."

"No! You have to help me!"

"Why?"

"You're my friend, and friends help each other, right?"

"Some friend you are," he said. "Every time I turn around, you're getting me into trouble."

63

"How about you? Every time I turn around, you're try-ing to make me mad," I told him.

He bounced the ball a few times.

"I need your help, Alphonso," I told him. "We can act like we're friends and help each other, or we can both get kicked out of school. What do you say?"

He tried to make a basket and missed.

"My basketball coach said it's all finesse," I said. "It's a small move," I knocked the ball from his hand and dribbled it back to the foul line. "A three-quarter turn of the wrist, like this."

Swish! The net barely moved as the ball cleared it. "That's your problem," I continued. "You don't understand the small moves. Everything's a grandstand when you play."

"Oh yeah? How are you going to finesse Uncle Buddy out of his movies?"

"You're right. Thanks, Alphonso."

"For what?"

"For being my friend. And reminding me to follow my own advice. Come on, and remember, back me up, no matter what. Just follow my lead. I'm going to introduce you to the soft sell."

We stopped for one last huddle before we went into

64

the barbershop. Strategy was everything in the soft sell. We rolled into the barbershop, trying our best to look casual.

"How was school today, Ella?" Uncle Buddy asked. He was busy giving a customer a trim.

"Great! We saw some old movies," Alphonso put in cheerfully. I made a face at him to remind him he was following *my* lead. After all, this was my mission.

"You wouldn't believe it, Uncle Buddy. Ms. Sewall showed us one of her old movies and told us all about Whitney Lloyd."

"Whitney Lloyd . . . hmm," said Mr. Simms. "I remember him. Supposed to be one of the handsomest Negro movie stars in the thirties."

"My Thelma would swoon at the sight of him. Thank heaven it was my arms she fell into," chuckled Mr. Perry.

Uncle Buddy clipped along at a steady pace. He didn't seem too interested.

"Ms. Sewall said he was the black Valentine," I continued.

"Valentino," corrected Uncle Buddy. Good. He was listening.

"I love the way he rode off at the end of what was it . . . *Flames? Fire?*" I asked innocently.

"*Fire on the Wind*," said Uncle Buddy, whipping the

65

drape off his customer. He took out the large, soft whisk broom and dusted away the stray hairs.

"That's it!" I cried excitedly. "He jumped off his horse in those fancy pants of his—"

"Jodhpurs! Ms. Sewall has a still photo of him in those," Alphonso added, getting just as excited as me.

". . . back straight as a board, head held high, right into the sunset. What a man!"

"What a ham!" muttered Uncle Buddy. He turned from the cash register and said firmly, "Whitney Lloyd was a two-bit actor with a high opinion of himself."

"Uncle Buddy, I told Ms. Sewall about the photo in the trunk. I told her you were twice as handsome as that old Whitney Lloyd." I moved in close, giving him a hug.

"And I bet you can act better than him, too," said Alphonso.

"Act, direct, produce, my uncle Buddy could do it all. And he did!"

"Tell us what it was like, Mr. Jackson," Alphonso said, pulling a chair close.

"Yeah, Uncle Buddy, tell us all about the stars."

Uncle Buddy looked over his glasses at us.

"What Whitney Lloyd needed . . . ," he paused for dramatic effect, and Alphonso and I leaned in closer, ". . . was the talent you two rascals have. Ella, there are towels to be folded and homework that has to get done. Get to it."

Our faces fell, our spirits sank. This was going to be harder than we thought.

I lay in bed that night, replaying in my mind what had happened in the barbershop that day, just like a director looking at dailies. I hated to admit it, but the soft sell hadn't worked. So much for small moves. It was time for the hard sell.

"What's the hard sell?" Alphonso asked as we walked home the next day.

"You throw everything you've got on the table. It's all or nothing."

"Suppose it's nothing?"

"Just think about Patrick Ewing giving that defense guy the elbow as he goes up in the air so he can get a foul."

"Got it. Hmm . . . the hard sell."

It took us two days to collect everything of value we owned.

We arrived at Uncle Buddy's barbershop with a full shopping bag. I pushed up my sleeves and reached into the bag.

"Okay. We're ready to do some serious business. One

movie . . . ," I stopped and conferred with Alphonso, ". . . *Lonesome Trail,* for our entire marble collection. Fourteen cat's-eyes!"

"How'd she get you into this, Alphonso?" asked Uncle Buddy.

"We're partners," Alphonso answered calmly.

"Partners in crime," Uncle Buddy replied.

Alphonso and I exchanged quick, guilty glances, wondering if he knew about Ms. Sewall's film. Nah . . . impossible.

Half an hour later the contents of the shopping bag were scattered about on the floor. Cap guns, dolls, posters, baseball mitts, an autographed baseball—everything we loved.

We made our last, and hopefully best, offer.

"A gift certificate personally signed by yours truly and . . ."

"Me truly, Alphonso Green . . ."

". . . entitling the bearer to one . . ."

". . . one entire *year* . . ."

". . . of inchworms, on demand . . ."

". . . big old, fat, juicy, wriggly inchworms . . ."

". . . personally dug up for your fishing convenience by the team of . . ."

". . . Green and Jackson."

68

"Jackson and Green."

"Mighty tempting," Uncle Buddy said slowly, "but . . ."

Mr. McKnight quietly passed us tickets.

"Two tickets to the Harry Belafonte concert at Constitution Hall," I said excitedly, yelping out my last offer.

"Harry who?" asked Alphonso.

"McKnight, stay out of this!" said Uncle Buddy.

"I can't stand your saying no to these kids, Buddy."

"You're all missing the point. Until a week ago I was a barber, and a good one. Since that blasted trunk arrived, everybody's been pestering me about something that happened sixty years ago.

"Who and what I am now doesn't seem to be good enough. So, friends, I don't want to hear one more question about those movies! End of story. Cut, print, it's a wrap."

SCENE 8

Dissolve: *A slow cut—as one picture fades away, a new one fades in. The director uses a dissolve to show that time has passed.*

"Sunset is just like a dissolve, isn't it, Uncle Buddy?"
I asked.

Friday after Thanksgiving was the day of the Turkey Bowl. Everyone in the neighborhood gathered for a game of touch football and a barbecue at Hains Point. Teams were divided up according to which side of the street you lived on. We bundled up in sweaters and played football until they called us for the last barbecued hot dogs and hamburgers we would eat until next June.

Hains Point was a piece of land that curled out into the Potomac River like a finger bent, saying "come here." If you stood at the farthest point—on the fingernail—faced the water, and looked straight ahead, it felt as if you were standing in the middle of the ocean.

The sun was beginning to set as the second game

wound down. Mom, Uncle Buddy, and I were sitting on a big rock at the tip of the point looking at the pink and orange ribbons in the sky.

"Uncle Buddy, when are you going to break down and show us your movies?" my mom said, out of the clear blue.

My mouth just about dropped to the ground.

"When you let us see your old college papers," said Uncle Buddy.

"Oh, it's not the same at all! My college papers are ancient history!"

"My point exactly!" he said. They laughed together because he had caught her with her own words. "My movies are ancient history," he said, smiling.

"And our history, black people's history, which has been taken from us since we were brought here as slaves, is too important to be swept under the rug and forgotten!"

"My rug, my broom, my movies," said Uncle Buddy.

"Brenda!" my dad called. "Can you help over here?" The game had ended, and everyone was starting to pack up.

"Coming," my mom yelled back. But before leaving she added, "If those movies were ancient history, you wouldn't have told them to Ella every night as bedtime stories. And don't you dare tell Joe that I said anything to you about them!"

"My lips are sealed," he promised.

"Yeah, too tightly!" said Mom with a laugh.

My uncle and I sat for a minute or two, not talking, just watching the changing colors. The pink and orange clouds looked wide and streaky, as if someone had taken an eraser to the sky.

"Sunset is just like a dissolve, isn't it, Uncle Buddy?" I asked.

Uncle Buddy looked at me with an odd expression, half pleased, half angry.

"Yes, but not everything's like a movie, Ella. I'm gonna tell you a story," he continued. My face must have lit up because he added, "No, not one of those. A true story. Starts in Chicago in 1928.

"Ella DuChamps and I had just finished making *Ways of the World*. So we hit the road to find places to show it."

"Why didn't you just show it in Chicago?"

"In those days all the movie houses in Chicago were owned by whites, and they got their movies from Hollywood. Those movies didn't use black actresses and actors for much more than maids and butlers. When there

72

was a movie about Negroes, we were made to look stupid or no good. But I wasn't from Hollywood, and my movies showed intelligent Negroes with ordinary lives and problems."

"How'd you figure out where to go to show your movies?"

"We found small towns with enough Negroes to fill a movie house. We pulled into Thomasville, Alabama. We met a man, I'll never forget his name, Tom Gibson. We worked out arrangements on how to split the gate."

"Gate?"

"The money from the tickets we sold. Ella and I put up posters, passed out flyers. Then, on a Wednesday night, black people poured out of nowhere and filled the theater."

"Why Wednesday? Why not a weekend?"

"Saturday was the big night for the white people to go to the movies, and on Sunday the black people were in church all day. We had at least three hundred people crammed in.

"Later, Ella and I go to this Mr. Gibson's office. He counts out ten dollars. I say, 'Where's the rest?' He says 'There ain't no rest, *boy*.' I knew I was in trouble because before that I had been 'William' to him.

73

"I say, 'There were three hundred people in here tonight!' I stood there a good five minutes, struggling to hold back my anger. Ella finally told him 'Thank you' and pulled me out of the office."

"He cheated you! Why didn't you tell the police?"

"Because he was white, and I was a black man bold enough to think of myself as an independent business-man. The police would have laughed in my face.

"So we took our movie and headed to the next town. And that's what the movie business was like."

We sat in silence for a while.

"So you quit movies because the man stole your money?"

"Well, no. There was more, Sugar. When I was in California—"

"California! You were in California! You mean like Hollywood, California? Uncle Buddy! You were in Hollywood?"

"You're gonna tell the whole city with that big mouth of yours," he said, and I quickly covered my mouth. It was so exciting, thinking about my uncle Buddy in Hollywood.

"Tell me what happened in Hollywood! Please!" I cried.

But before Uncle Buddy could say anything, he got that kind of sad, funny look on his face again, like he wanted to cry. It made me feel a little strange inside. How can something exciting like being in Hollywood make you feel bad?

"I just don't want to talk about it," Uncle Buddy said. He pulled a handkerchief from his sweater pocket and wiped his face with it. He wasn't sweating, so it must have been tears.

He stood up and walked off toward the car. He and my mom folded up the card table.

I sat there, chewing on my lip, hoping that someday he would finish the story. It was so hard to understand. If I were in Hollywood, it would be like a dream come true. Why hadn't it been a dream come true for Uncle Buddy?

"Ella! Let's go!" Dad called.

As we climbed into the backseat of the car, I reached over and tapped Uncle Buddy on the arm. I asked quietly, "Even though it didn't work out so good, are you glad you made those movies anyway?"

"Yes, Ella. Yes, I am."

"Me, too," I said with a big grin.

SCENE 9

Reaction Shot: *There are two people in the scene, but we only see one as he or she speaks. After that person speaks, the director cuts to the person who is listening to see how he or she feels about what has been said.*

"And these reaction shots with Ella DuChamps! How in the world did he do that with only one camera?"

Left, left, left, right, right, up, down, left. Sometimes life was just like one of those hand-held pinball games. You keep tilting the thing, but just as two balls go in, one comes out.

Alphonso and I were friends again, but he was sure to get a bad grade in Ms. Sewall's class, since I had ruined her film and he was my partner.

Mom thought Uncle Buddy should share his movies with the world because they were a part of African American history, but Dad and Uncle Buddy didn't want to hear a word about movies.

Ms. Sewall was very excited about Uncle Buddy's movies but still looked tired and sad in class—which may have something to do with my firebombing her movie.

Left, right, left, left, left . . . Rats.

How could I get all the balls to go into the hole?

All it would take was one powerful ball. I had to pull back the hammer with all my might and send that baby bouncing off the walls with so much speed and energy that the quick left, left, right, sent it spinning around that hole and then straight in.

I would take one of Uncle Buddy's films and give it to Ms. Sewall.

Thursday afternoon I sat at my desk in the barbershop trying to concentrate on my math homework. My mind kept wandering to the trunk sitting in the back room. For days I had imagined myself tiptoeing into the room, opening the trunk, and taking out one of the film cans.

Suppose I got caught? When I first got the idea, I felt a cold fist in the middle of my stomach. Then, as I imagined Uncle Buddy at the gala, taking bows and getting a standing ovation from the audience, my stomach began to feel better and the fist went away.

My eyes filled with tears, and I got goose bumps up

and down my arms as the sheer thrill of my plan swept over me. I would secretly give Ms. Sewall one of Uncle Buddy's films—that was the one powerful shot that would win the game. Even Uncle Buddy would eventually thank me.

I drummed my pencil on the desk. Uncle Buddy was outside sweeping the sidewalk. Mrs. Velaquez, owner of *Editorial el Mundo*, came out and started talking to him.

There were no customers in the barbershop.

Slowly I tiptoed to the back room. The floor creaked. I held my finger up to my lips to say "*Shh*" and noticed that my hands were so stiff and wet that I could barely close them. Suppose I dropped the film? Uncle Buddy would come rushing in, see me, call the police . . .

Stop! This is not the time to let your imagination run away with you, I told myself.

I rubbed my hands against my jeans and shook them out. Mrs. Velaquez was talking about her sister, who was coming to visit from Panama. There was still time.

Finally I was in the back room. Yipes! Where was the trunk? My eyes scanned the room like radar looking for a submarine. There it was! Someone had thrown a blanket over it.

78

I pulled the blanket off and opened the trunk. There they were. Left, right . . .

"All right, Mrs. V., I'll be seeing you," I heard Uncle Buddy say.

Leffttt! Oh my gosh! He was coming!

"Oh, Mr. Jackson, one more thing. My nephew Alejandro, the barber, is thinking about going into business for himself, and I was wondering if you could talk to him. . . ."

"Why, sure, I'd love to speak to him."

Aaaaahhhhh! It was now or never!

The hinges gave a loud creak as I opened the trunk. I reached inside and quickly took out a reel. I dashed back to my desk and placed it in my backpack. I could breathe again.

I forgot to put the blanket back over the trunk!

Mrs. V. was leaving. Uncle Buddy turned to come into the barbershop. I'd never known what the expression "cold sweat" meant until now. He looked down at the sidewalk and stopped. He started sweeping again.

I dashed into the back room and threw the blanket over the trunk. Uncle Buddy was still sweeping when I made it back to my seat.

That night I dreamed about a giant pinball game. I was

inside, and the object of the game was to knock me over with the giant balls.

The next day, I hung around the media center until all the other students had left. Ms. Sewall was busy erasing the board and didn't see me take the film can out of my backpack.

"Oh. What's this?" she asked, turning to me and brushing chalk dust from her hands.

I silently offered the film can to her.

"Ella! He finally agreed!" Ms. Sewall gave a little yelp of delight and carefully took the can away from me.

My mouth opened to tell her what I had done, but no words came out. I followed Ms. Sewall to the lab countertop, where she turned on bright lights and set down the film can.

"Ella, this is a historic moment. This is the most important thing that has ever happened to me in my career. *Hmmmm* . . . this brown stuff around the edge is nitrate deterioration. I've told you about this before. It's natural. It tells us the film might not be in tip-top shape."

With great care, Ms. Sewall pried open the can. Inside there was only a heap of dusty brown powder.

She was disappointed. I was crushed.

"You've got to expect things like this. After all, this has been sitting unpreserved for fifty years. But you said there were lots of cans. Maybe your uncle Buddy can send several more over—even though I know he hates to part with them."

"More than you realize," I muttered under my breath.

"I'll give him a call. What's his number?"

"No! No, Ms. Sewall. He's . . . he's got a doctor's appointment today. I'll just tell him what happened when I see him this afternoon. I'm sure it won't be a problem."

"Great. And thanks so much, Ella, for helping him understand how important his films really are—not just to me, but to the world. You're a peach!"

Tonight those giant pinballs would have faces on them. With big, ugly teeth. And they would be even faster than before. I'd never get to sleep if I took another film, and I'd never get to sleep if I didn't.

The next afternoon all the regulars were in the barber-shop. I was sure I wouldn't get a chance to get to the trunk. But finally they packed up the chess game, and I gave a sigh of relief as they stepped outside to finish up their coffee and conversation.

81

I looked at the contents of the trunk a bit more carefully this time, hoping to find a reel with no brown stuff at all on the outside. I moved aside a pack of letters tied with a ribbon. As I moved it, I saw the name W. B. Jackson in the upper left corner of the envelope where the return address is written.

"*Hmmm*, 'W. B. Jackson, 842 Los Feliz Boulevard, Hollywood, California, 2.' I wonder how long Uncle Buddy lived in Hollywood?" With a frown, I slowly laid it aside and found two reels I thought might be lucky ones.

"This is it!" cried Ms. Sewall, holding up a piece of film between two white-gloved fingers.

"Is it? Really?" I laughed, limp with relief.

"He's going to be thrilled when he sees this all polished and shined up!"

There it was. Another moment when I could tell the truth.

"Ms. Sewall . . . Uncle Buddy—"

". . . is a genius!"

"But he doesn't even—"

". . . realize how fabulous these are. Just wait till he sees this little diamond after I get it transferred to videocassette. His heart will melt."

82

"But Ms. Sewall, listen."

Ms. Sewall went to the machine called the Steenbeck and slowly and respectfully threaded the film. I felt like I was in church.

"Whitney Lloyd! Oh my gosh, this must have been his first film appearance. Look at the quality of the lighting! And these reaction shots with Ella DuChamps! How in the world did he do that with only one camera? It must have taken him days to move the camera from one position to another, keeping the light the same so it would look as smooth as it does. Hardly any damage at all. A miracle . . ."

I slowly left the room, knowing that I was the one who needed the miracle.

SCENE 10

Zoom: *In a zoom shot, the camera moves quickly toward what it is shooting.*

"Alphonso? Alphonso, you just zoomed in on my feet."

---

had heard the expression "Two wrongs don't make a right" and was considering my odds of getting one wrong to make a right. Fat chance, I thought.

Even though Ms. Sewall was her usual cheery self, I couldn't get interested in her class today. I sat slumped at my desk. Alphonso passed by and bumped into my books, knocking them to the floor. I didn't move. I didn't even open my mouth.

Surprised, he backed up a few steps to see if it was really me, before giving a shrug and sitting down.

"All right, settle down, folks," said Ms. Sewall. "The teams that have finished their list of subjects and have their parental permission slips can come up and get their cameras."

Ordinarily I would have been first in line to get

my hands on a real movie camera. But I looked at the line and turned away, and Alphonso took up a place at the end.

"I want you to remember everything I've taught you about handling a camera," Ms. Sewall said, moving from team to team giving last-minute tips. "Yours for the weekend, but I'll expect them back in the lab in tip-top condition on Monday morning. Class dismissed, and remember, you're my little video cadets!"

"Ms. Sewall," blared the P.A. system. "Please report to the office; you have a visitor." Ms. Sewall left the room with the students as the bell rang.

Only Alphonso and I were left.

"So. You want to carry it home first?" he offered.

"Nope."

"What's wrong with you?"

"I took two of Uncle Buddy's films and gave them to Ms. Sewall," I admitted, glad to be able to say it out loud. I saw Alphonso's eyes get big.

"You mean you stole them?"

I sat up straight, rigid with indignation and anger. *Stole!* How could he use that word? Because it was true. I sagged back into my seat. "Yeah."

"Dag. And you're usually a Goody Two-shoes."

85

"If only I could get him to change his mind about the movies."

"At first," Alphonso said, sitting on a desktop, "you think taking something you want will make it better for you, you know, make you feel good. So how come it makes you feel so rotten?"

"Yeah."

"We're dead meat when Ms. Sewall finds out you stole that movie you gave her."

"We?"

"Yeah. 'We.' Taking the movies, that took guts. It was a bold move, but stupid. Like when Butch and Sundance jumped off the cliff into the river when the posse was after them," he said.

"You've seen *Butch Cassidy and the Sundance Kid*?" I asked, surprised.

"Yeah, it was on last Sunday on the *Channel Five Matinee*."

I wasn't sure I liked the idea of being bold but stupid. Still, it was nice having someone around who understood both my good and bad qualities and still liked me.

"Thanks, Butch," I said.

"No problem, Sundance. Just appreciate that you'll have some company when you jump."

"Yeah, and my parents will be leading the posse, trying to shoot us even after we've hit the water. My parents! Oh man, it's over. Unless . . ."

"What?"

"Unless," I said, my voice getting squeaky with excitement as I picked up the video camera, "we can get Uncle Buddy to really remember what it feels like to be a director! And I think this is the baby that will help us! Come on, Alphonso!"

I backed into the barbershop, followed by Alphonso, camera clumsily sitting on his shoulder.

"Lights! Roll tape! Action! We're here in Jackson's Barbershop," I said in my best news-reporter voice. "Alphonso? Alphonso, you just zoomed in on my feet."

"Sorry. I keep forgetting to look through the little hole when I push the red button."

Uncle Buddy, playing checkers, gave only a brief glance in our direction, and then said, "King me," to Mr. McKnight.

"Hey, are we gonna be movie stars?" asked Mr. Simms, putting down his newspaper.

"Don't point that thing at him, I'm telling you, he'll break it!" warned Mr. McKnight.

"Look at how tiny the camera is! You see that, Buddy?" Mr. Perry exclaimed in amazement.

"What should we shoot?" I asked.

"Why not Mr. Simms?" Alphonso offered.

Nervously, Mr. Simms brushed off the shoulders of his jacket and straightened his tie. He cleared his throat loudly, then smiled for the camera.

"Hi. Do you know me? My name, uh, my name is . . ."

"Lord, he's forgotten his name!" Mr. Perry cackled.

"Shut up, Perry! My name is Leo Simms," he said. "I'm a native of Washington, D.C., and I've been here all my life except the two years I served in World War II."

I watched Uncle Buddy from the corner of my eye as I asked Mr. Simms questions about his family. He was interested—I could tell. He started to cut a customer's hair.

"I've got a wife, Janie, and all five of my children live here, nine grandchildren . . ."

"Make sure you keep the camera up, Alphonso," I said. Uncle Buddy had stopped cutting hair and was watching what was going on.

"Why don't you move him to the left so you'll have more backlight?" Uncle Buddy suggested.

Alphonso and I looked at each other. The plan was working.

88

Alphonso lowered the camera while I moved Mr. Simms to a better position.

"Gosh, that thing makes me nervous," said Mr. Simms.

"Here, let me talk to it," said Mr. Perry, taking his place.

"Wait a minute," said Uncle Buddy just as Alphonso was about to shoot. He guided Alphonso over to a barber chair, sat him in it, pushed the bar to move him up, and angled him.

"Now shoot," he said.

"Wait a minute, Alphonso," I said. "We're supposed to be shooting an action. It says so right here on our assignment sheet."

"Maybe we can shoot the barbershop pole. That's moving."

Uncle Buddy frowned.

"I don't know," I said. "How about if Mr. McKnight walks in the door?"

Uncle Buddy moved his head back and forth in a "maybe" sort of way.

"Sure I can walk for you; I'm a fine walker!" added Mr. McKnight.

"Since you're in a barbershop, why don't you shoot Mr. McKnight getting a *haircut*?" suggested Uncle Buddy.

89

Bingo! Alphonso and I grinned at each other. We spent the next half hour shooting a haircut. Uncle Buddy talked about when he became a barber and how he learned to do the styles with the sharply cut lines and letters.

We're on a real shoot, I thought happily. Uncle Buddy was terrific, helping us with the light, adjusting the shades, moving the chair about, telling us when to zoom in, when to shoot long and wide.

He was amazed at the lightness of the camera and excited to be able to see the actual picture we had just taken, right there on the instant replay.

Finally we were finished. Mr. McKnight had a haircut, and we had some great footage.

Uncle Buddy carefully put away his brushes and scissors, and Alphonso and I swept the floor clean.

"You better get along, Miss Ella. Your dad's sure to have dinner on the table by now," Uncle Buddy said.

We packed up the camera and slowly headed for the door.

"That teacher of yours still want to see my work?"

I nodded, holding my breath.

"*Hmm*. Tell her I'll bring in the trunk on Monday."

Alphonso and I did a high five and bolted out the door.

That night I scooted down under my blanket, feeling relieved, cozy, and warm. I had finally gotten Uncle Buddy to share his movies.

With a yawn, I reminded myself to tell Ms. Sewall that Uncle Buddy didn't know about my burning up her movie, or giving her one of his movies, then a second one. Oh, there was a lot to explain, but I was sure Ms. Sewall would understand.

Finally I could tell the truth. What a relief! Everything was going to be A-OK. Left, left, right, left, and look at that baby spin and sink! Yes!

SCENE 11

Close-up: *The camera lens shoots very close to the object or actor, so that it appears very large on the screen.*

By now my face was so close to the plate that the spaghetti looked like a close-up of the squirming tentacles of some strange Martian creature.

I swung into the kitchen and gave Dad a bear hug so tight he almost dropped the big wooden spoon dripping with spaghetti sauce.

"My, my, I haven't seen you this happy in weeks." He watched as I cheerfully pulled out the silverware and place mats to set the table—without being asked!

"It's because we're having *spaghetti* tonight! My absolutely, positively favorite meal," I almost sang as I skipped into the dining room.

As he put the big platter of spaghetti on the table, Mom walked in the door.

"Sorry, I'm late, folks. We had a real emergency

with one of our new mothers just before my shift ended," she called from the kitchen as she washed her hands.

"Well, your emergency is taken care of and you're just in time for my announcement," said Uncle Buddy, entering the dining room. He wouldn't tell us anything until after we sat down and said grace.

"What is it?" Mom asked. She started serving the spaghetti.

"I know I said that my movie days were behind me," Uncle Buddy began, "and I didn't want to talk about it, but Ella's been working on me."

Dad shot me a warning glance.

"And I've decided that it would be a good idea to let Ms. Sewall take a look at my movies."

"Uncle Buddy! That's great!" Mom said.

You don't know how great, I thought to myself.

Mom began to talk fast, shooting questions at Uncle Buddy. The doorbell rang and Dad got up to get it. He looked surprised when he came back to the dining room with Ms. Sewall.

I was shocked.

"I didn't mean to interrupt your dinner," she said, reaching for Dad's hand. "I'm Ricki Sewall, and Mrs.

Jackson, I remember you from Career Day. I'm Ella's media lab teacher, remember?"

"Oh, yes," said Mom, "we were just talking about you. Would you care to join us for dinner?"

"No, but thank you for the offer," Ms. Sewall said.

I noticed Uncle Buddy rising out of his chair to greet her, and suddenly the pattern on my plate looked very interesting to me. Oh boy, oh boy, oh boy, was the only thought my mind could form. I could barely hear their conversation.

One word kept ringing in my head over and over again—*Thief! Thief! Thief!*

Ms. Sewall's eyes grew wide as she reached for Uncle Buddy's hand and started pumping it up and down.

"Oh, Mr. Jackson, Mr. W. B. Jackson, sir, you have no idea what an incredible honor it is to meet you!" Uncle Buddy's arm was getting tired, so Dad offered Ms. Sewall a chair.

"I'm sorry, I need to explain why I'm here," she said, flustered. "I just started transferring . . ."

Oh boy, oh boy, oh boy, I repeated silently. By now my face was so close to the plate that the spaghetti looked like a close-up of the squirming tentacles of some strange Martian creature. Oh boy, oh boy, oh boy.

94

". . . to videocassette the first film you gave Ella, and I couldn't stay away a moment longer."

"The what I gave Ella?" asked Uncle Buddy, completely surprised.

"The movie," said Ms. Sewall. *Flames of Wrath.* I couldn't stay away. This discovery will set the film world on its ear. Ella said you were reluctant to talk about the films, but I had to come and meet you anyway."

The room was so quiet you could hear a pin drop. Everyone turned to me. I wished Scotty could beam me up.

"Oh boy," were the two words that actually came from my lips.

"Is something wrong?" Ms. Sewall asked uneasily.

"Oh boy."

"Ella, you've got some explaining to do," said Dad sternly.

"I should say so," Mom put in. "How did Ms. Sewall get Uncle Buddy's movie?" she asked. "Did you give it to her without Uncle Buddy's permission?"

"Yes." It was a yes so quiet you could barely hear it.

"Oh, Ella," said Uncle Buddy.

"Oh boy," said Ms. Sewall.

"I'm sorry," I wailed, tears spilling from my eyes, "but it all got so confused."

"Let's clear it up now," Dad ordered in a steely voice.

"Well, first Ms. Sewall had her own movie and we were going to take a picture and the bottle of acid stuff spilled on it and there was this smoke . . ."

"Acid! Smoke!" exclaimed Mom.

". . . and her film was gone. All of it. So then I sort of told her Uncle Buddy would let her see his old movie. I felt so bad because I had messed up her movie. Then Uncle Buddy didn't want to give up his movie, so I . . . I . . . I took them because I knew, I just knew he would change his mind and then the whole world would know about the great things he'd done, and Ms. Sewall would have an old movie to show at the gala."

No one said anything for a long time.

"Ella, you told me he *wanted* to share his work!" said Ms. Sewall.

"I didn't exactly say that—"

"You have let your imagination run away with you one time too many, young lady," Dad scolded. "Those films are Uncle Buddy's, to do with as he pleases. They don't belong to us—or Ms. Sewall."

"You let things snowball, Ella!" added Mom. "Why didn't you tell us about Ms. Sewall's film being ruined?"

"I don't know! I just knew I could get Uncle Buddy to love his movies again. It seemed like a good idea when I had it. I don't understand how things got so confused."

"I think you should go to your room now," Mom said in a low voice, "and take some time to think about what you did."

I left the room slowly, tears running down my face. For the next twenty minutes I heard the rise and fall of adult voices from below, but I couldn't even bear to go to the top of the stairs to eavesdrop.

SCENE 12

Music Cue: *A music cue marks the beginning of a speech or action. Music cues can predict a coming event, establish or change a mood, or tell us about the personality of a character we are watching.*

"Listen, if we back this up by forty frames for the music cue, we'll be able to get the first big beat right as the kids start to cross the street," Alphonso said, leaning in close to the monitor.

I t's been three days now since Mom and Dad grounded me. My sentence is one month—a whole month!—without phone calls, my favorite television shows, practicing basketball, playing with friends, or going to the barbershop after school. A week ago, I never would have thought it would be a big deal not hanging out with Alphonso for a month. But now I miss him. And I can't even attend the gala for the premiere of our video-class projects!

At first I handled it okay. After all, it's just beginning to get cold outside, and it's been icy a lot, too. And I don't

98

really watch that much television anyway—most of the stuff I like comes on when I'm supposed to be in bed. And the gala—oh yeah. Missing that will be hard, but I'll live.

But more than being grounded, more than no Alphonso, no basketball, no more weekday matinees, and no gala, I hate not talking to Uncle Buddy. I want to talk to him, but whenever I see him—sitting in the living room, walking down the hall, at breakfast and dinner—he acts like I'm not there. He doesn't even look at me. I thought he would be mad for a little while, but then everything would be okay. But he's still mad. The most he has said to me in three days is "Pass the broccoli" at dinner, and even then he didn't look at me. I have this weird, sick feeling in my stomach that doesn't go away. I believe Uncle Buddy hates me.

Yesterday Uncle Buddy didn't even go to his barbershop. He kept it closed all day while he sat in his room listening to his Billie Holiday records. The same songs, over and over again. Mom said I shouldn't worry, that Uncle Buddy was "a little depressed and needs some time to himself." But I don't think he's depressed at all. I think he hates me and hates living in the same house with me.

"Funny," my mom commented this morning before I went off to school, "how one little decision can change

99

your whole life." I had heard her say that before, but I never understood its real meaning until now.

"I wish I could just go back and change it all," I told her.

Mom opened her arms and I fell into her hug. "You can't," she said. "You can only try to make up for it."

"I told Uncle Buddy I was sorry, almost a hundred times, but he still won't talk to me."

"Then you'll just have to wait until he's ready." She gave me a kiss on the forehead. I was just starting to feel a little better when Uncle Buddy walked in. He saw me and turned right back around. That odd, sick feeling in my stomach returned.

"Listen, if we back this up by forty frames for the music cue, we'll be able to get the first big beat right as the kids start to cross the street," Alphonso said, leaning in close to the monitor.

"Whatever," I replied. I wasn't really interested in finishing the video. All I could think about was Uncle Buddy.

"How long are you gonna mope around, Ella? It was a bold move, but you got caught. Get over it!"

"That's easy for you to say. You can still go to the barbershop!"

"Yeah." He laughed. "You should have heard the story Mr. Simms told about this bear . . ."

He didn't finish his sentence. He must have seen he was making me feel worse.

"Look," Alphonso said, "we're almost done with this. Let's just get it over with."

"Yeah," I said. "Because when we're finished with this, I'm never making another video ever again."

We spent the whole week laying down the sound track for our video. Alphonso was doing a great job. I knew exactly what song I wanted, but I couldn't remember the title. After I hummed a few bars, Ms. Sewall recognized the tune and loaned us "As Time Goes By," from the movie *Casablanca*. We were using it at the beginning and end of our movie, *Saturday at Jackson's Barbershop*.

The next week we spent doing character generation—putting the words on the screen. It's a funny name, but each letter is called a character. We worked really hard on the movie. We got the chance to watch the video a few times to make sure we were satisfied with what we had done. Uncle Buddy was smiling in our movie, but when I thought about his sad face lately, I never wanted to see this—or any other movie—again. But I wasn't going to

101

make things worse by making Alphonso get a bad grade from Ms. Sewall.

We turned our video in to Ms. Sewall right on time. "Your tape will be the first one I watch," she said with a smile.

On the last day before Christmas vacation, Ms. Sewall brought chocolate Santas, and we decorated a tree using the Polaroid pictures we shot way back in September. Ms. Sewall took a Polaroid of Juanita, Renee, Debra, and me wearing elf hats, and added it to the tree. It was the strangest-looking Christmas tree I ever saw, but I liked it.

"I want to take a moment to say 'Well done' to all of you," Ms. Sewall began, glancing at the clock. It was almost time for the bell to ring, for our vacation to begin.

"I have so much I want to say. First of all, I want to thank you. I've had a marvelous time with you. I'd never thought of myself as a teacher before, but I had always wanted to pass along to others what I'd learned. Thank you for giving me the chance to do that. I think we should give ourselves a hand."

Everyone applauded. Alphonso stood up and took a bow. I clapped, but not as hard as the others.

"I've already had a chance to look at your videos. And

I can tell by the work you've done that you have learned so much about making movies. I want you all to go beyond this class and continue to tell stories that are important to you, and to tell them in your own unique way." She wiped tears from her eyes.

"So next time I see you, you'll all be in your party dresses and best suits at the gala!" The bell rang. The last media lab class was finished. "Merry Christmas, everybody!" she shouted as we ran out the doors.

"Could you two wait a minute?" Ms. Sewall asked Alphonso and me as we were heading for the door.

Uh-oh, the responsibility and honesty speech, I thought.

"I wanted to give you your grades," she said instead.

Alphonso looked as uncomfortable as I felt. "But shouldn't we wait for report cards?" he asked.

"Usually. But I really wanted to be around to share this with you two." She gave us each an envelope.

I opened mine, and my eyes got wide. Alphonso saw the look on my face and tore his open.

"An A!" he screamed. "I don't believe it! Yippee!" He jumped all around the room.

I looked at my A again, not believing it was real.

"This must be a mistake," I said, my voice sounding

103

kind of froggy because I was about to cry. "I mean, we ruined your movie."

"I've been watching the two of you. You've done some fine work in this class. And I'm especially proud of you because you persevered even after all the disasters. You could have given up, but you didn't."

You could have given up, but you didn't. Those words rang in my head the whole way home. I *did* go through a lot to make that video. Yes, most of the trouble had been my fault, but still, Ms. Sewall was right. I had made the decision to keep going. The other words I thought about were my mother's: "Funny how one little decision can change your whole life." Uncle Buddy had made a decision, too, and because of it, he's a barber now. A very good barber, but it's not what he was a long time ago. He gave up. It must have been a lot of trouble to make him give up something as wonderful as filmmaking.

We went to my aunt Esther's for Christmas dinner. There were about thirty uncles, aunts, cousins, and friends there. Three tables were set up, and I was in charge of the punch bowl, pouring ginger ale as needed over the big block of frozen juice thick with cherries and slices of oranges and limes.

104

Every now and then I caught bits and pieces of soft conversations between adults that included the words "trunk full of movies" and "Hollywood." They would glance over their shoulders to make sure that Uncle Buddy wasn't nearby. I knew the movies were important—and so did the rest of our family. Why didn't Uncle Buddy see it that way?

When we got home that night, Mom and Dad went to bed early and encouraged me to do the same. But I just couldn't sleep. There were still toys I wanted to play with under the tree and clothes to try on. So when it was quiet, I crept out of bed, put on my robe and slippers, and tip-toed downstairs to find a doll or the math safari game to bring back to my room. I wasn't the only person awake.

Uncle Buddy was sitting at the dining-room table in his robe and pajamas. I guess he couldn't sleep, either. He looked up and saw me, but instead of turning away mad, he gave me a little bit of a smile.

"Merry Christmas, Ella," he said.

"Merry Christmas, Uncle Buddy."

I noticed that sitting right in front of him, on the table, was an unopened gift. It was a big square box—I couldn't even guess what was in it. I asked Uncle Buddy if he forgot to unwrap it this morning, and who gave it to him.

"Oh, this isn't for me, Ella. It's from me to you."

I heard myself gasp just a little. He had already given me a gift—a Kenya doll and a pair of thick knee-highs. And when I had thanked him with a kiss, he'd smiled only a little, not the way he used to, back when he still loved me.

He pushed the gift across the table to me. I reached out and pulled off the foil wrapping to find a plain brown box underneath. I removed the top and heard myself gasp again—this time a big gasp. In the box were four reels of film from Uncle Buddy's trunk! The labels on the reels said *Heavenly Hostess* and *Flames of Wrath*.

"I've been thinking a lot about what you did. Even though taking my movies was wrong, I understand why you did it. And if you still think these old things can do somebody some good, if you still believe there's anybody out there who would want to see them, you go on and have that teacher of yours clean them up and put them on video, or whatever she wants to do. Just remember to return them when you're done."

I couldn't speak. Tears were running down my face so quickly I couldn't wipe them away fast enough. I threw my arms around Uncle Buddy's neck and hugged him so hard I thought my arms would break.

He hugged me and patted my back. "I thought you

106

hated me!" I cried, sobbing into his shoulder.

"Hated you? Ella, I could never hate you. I was mad at you, yes. But I could never hate you."

I pulled away to look at his face, to see if he was telling the truth. He was. He was smiling his old smile at me again.

"Then what made you decide to let Ms. Sewall have your movies?"

"Time and again I've heard your mother say, 'Funny how one little decision can change your whole life.'

"I made a decision like that a long time ago. It didn't seem so big then. But it's caused me way too much grief. There's no reason you should be unhappy because of something I did sixty years ago. Maybe giving you the films will help make up for it."

"Why won't you tell me why you stopped making movies?"

"It hurts too much. I will tell you this. I gave up my dream. When you give up your dream, you give up a big piece of your life. Never, never give up your dream. If you want to make movies, Ella, then you go right on out there and make whatever kind of movies you want. You do what you have to do to follow your dream. Promise me."

"I promise," I said, wiping away another tear. Uncle

107

Buddy kissed my forehead. "I also promise I'll never do anything to make you that mad at me again."

"That's all in the past now. Tomorrow we're gonna find a way to get in touch with that teacher of yours and get her these films. And you tell her there's more where these came from! Wait until they take a look at *Flames of Wrath* at that gala next month."

"But Mom and Dad said I can't go!"

Uncle Buddy smiled. "We'll see about that."

SCENE 13

Steenbeck: *A Steenbeck is a machine used to repair and to edit a film. It is a table with two reels for the film and a small TV screen between the reels. When you edit a movie, you cut or add pictures to it. You can look at the film frame by frame and find the exact place to cut or add to the film.*

When I came back, the lights were low and Ms. Sewall was hunched over the Steenbeck, slowly winding a film clip through it.

It was below zero when I woke up that first school day after Christmas vacation. It was clear and sunny, and the morning sunshine coming through the half-moon window over the front door made my favorite pattern on the stairs to the second floor. I always made sure to jump around the pattern when I walked up the stairs. I thought of it as my own personal rainbow.

It was a rainbow kind of morning. Uncle Buddy

was going to school with me to take the films to Ms. Sewall.

"Get an extra sweater and those leg things of yours, Ella," he said as he pulled on his coat. I ran up the stairs to get my leg warmers and the sweater, careful not to step on my rainbow. As I came down, Mom was opening the front door, coming in from the night shift.

"Hey, Mom!" I called. "I got your scarf, too, Uncle Buddy." I stood on the last step and reached up, tying it around his neck.

"Where are you two headed?" Mom asked in surprise.

"To school," I answered.

"I know where you're headed, Ella, but Uncle Buddy, the shop doesn't open until noon. Where are you on your way to? It's awful cold out there."

"To school," he said.

Mom's eyes got big.

"Oh no, what has she done now? Has something happened?"

"Mo-o-o-o-m!" I giggled.

"Nothing like that," said Uncle Buddy. "She can't carry these big cans of films by herself, so I'm going with her."

That really surprised Mom. She looked from Buddy to me and knew that we had made up.

"And the films are for . . . ," she said slowly.

"Ms. Sewall to clean up," finished Uncle Buddy.

She just stood there a minute, looking pleased.

"Mom, we're getting hot," I said.

"And we don't want to be tardy," added Uncle Buddy.

She opened the door and was still standing there when I glanced back, just before we turned the corner. I waved one more time. For some reason, I wanted her to stand there forever.

I felt very important walking into school with my uncle Buddy and the box of films. We went to Mrs. Henderson's room, and Uncle Buddy asked permission for me to go to see Ms. Sewall with him. Mrs. Henderson agreed, although I bet she thought I was in trouble again. Alphonso was coming in as we left and gave Uncle Buddy a high five.

"We're going to give Ms. Sewall the films!" I squeaked.

"Oh, man, can I come, too?"

"No you cannot, Mr. Alphonso, it's 8:50," said Mrs. Henderson, stepping out into the hall.

We went downstairs to the media center. Ms. Sewall wasn't there. Uncle Buddy took the film canisters out of

111

the box and stacked them on the lab table. He noticed the Steenbeck and went over to it.

"It's been a long time since I've seen one of these. They're a lot fancier now, but I see the same company still makes them."

"I know how to use it! Want me to show you?" I said.

He looked surprised and kind of pleased, too. *Tickled*—that's the word he would use. But before he could answer, Ms. Sewall came in.

"Ella, Mr. Jackson—what a surprise! Oh!"

"Ms. Sewall, Ms. Sewall! Guess what!" I cried. "Uncle Buddy's going to let you clean up some of his movies!"

Ms. Sewall sat down quickly.

Uncle Buddy took the movies out of the canisters.

"*Flames of Wrath* and *Heavenly Hostess*," he announced.

Ms. Sewall burst into tears.

Oh, no, I thought. Did I do something wrong?

"Ms. Sewall, please don't cry!" I said.

"Ella, I'm crying because this is such an important moment. This is history! Can I hug you, Mr. Jackson?"

She gave Uncle Buddy a bear hug, then gave me one, too. That's when I knew everything was going to be all right.

Ms. Sewall worked very hard on the movies. I saw her

in the media lab first thing in the morning, and she was still there when Dad picked me up from aftercare. Twice, Uncle Buddy came to school to watch and talk to her as she worked with the film.

The gala was only a week away. Ms. Sewall had just started the second film that Uncle Buddy had given her.

"Ella," she called to me as the bell rang and the class filed out the door. "Can you stay and help me clean up the room? I've got to get started on this next clip, and I don't have much time. I want to send the finished film and the first three minutes of the second one home with you this afternoon for Mr. Jackson to see. I want him to look at them before the gala."

She gave me a note, excusing my tardiness, to take to the aftercare program. When I came back, the lights were low and Ms. Sewall was hunched over the Steenbeck, slowly winding a film clip through it. I began to pick books off the floor and straighten desks. I was near the part of the room with the Steenbeck, and I couldn't help stopping to look over her shoulder.

At first it was funny. As the film ran—a little slowly because of the film speed—a black man with big ears and a shiny head raised his hands over his head and

113

waved them happily. He was in a field. He gave a big laugh and you could see that a lot of his front teeth were missing. He ran through the field, looking for something. He found it. It was a huge watermelon. He sure was glad to see that watermelon. His eyes rolled around, and he licked his lips. Finally he pulled out his pocket knife, cut the watermelon open, and dug his face into it.

I felt embarrassed and ashamed. The man was supposed to be ridiculous, laughable—just because his skin was black. I had never seen black people on television or in movies act that way. Nobody I knew acted that way.

I knew I should get the rest of the room cleaned up, but I couldn't move. I kept watching. The shadow of two huge wings appeared over the man's head, and he looked up, scared to death. A big white man with a white robe and long, white wavy hair hovered over him like a helicopter. He shook his finger at him like he was a bad little boy, and the black man cried and fell on his knees, begging for mercy. The white man was supposed to be an angel from heaven, I guess. Oh my gosh—*this* was *Heavenly Hostess*! *This* was Uncle Buddy's movie!

114

Ms. Sewall stopped the machine. "Wow. What a shame, no wonder he left Hollywood and disappeared." She rubbed her eyes and stretched. "Can you turn the lights on for me, Ella?"

I walked over and turned on the lights.

"What's wrong?" Ms. Sewall asked. I guess she could tell by my face that I was unhappy.

"I . . . I . . . ," I stammered. "I've got to go . . . see you, Ms. Sewall." I ran out of the room and down to aftercare.

I pulled out my notebook to start my homework. But I just stared at the page. Instead of words, I kept seeing the man eating the watermelon and cowering before the angel.

"What's the deal?"

I heard Alphonso's voice and slammed the book shut, thinking he could see inside my head.

"Nothing," I mumbled.

"So, you gonna ask your parents if you can go to the gala?"

"Nope," I answered, and got up to get today's snack, fruit punch and chocolate graham crackers, from the aftercare aide. Alphonso followed me and grabbed a snack, too—his second or third one, by the look from the aide.

"Why not?"

"It's part of my punishment, remember?"

"Yeah, but since Uncle Buddy gave up the films, I bet they'll want you to be there to see them."

"So who wants to see them?" I said under my breath.

"What?" Alphonso finished eating his graham crackers and looked at me suspiciously.

"You want that?" he said, pointing to my crackers. I shook my head.

"How come you don't want to see the movies all of a sudden? I mean you got into all this trouble in the first place because you wanted to see them so badly."

"Well, I saw them, okay!" I burst out. "And they're stupid. Some ugly man eating watermelon. They're just plain stupid. I don't ever want to talk about them again."

"So you're not going to the gala and you're not ever going to talk about them to your Uncle Buddy 'cause you didn't like the movie?"

"Right." I rested my head on the desk.

I stayed that way for ten minutes, and I thought Alphonso had gone away. I finally sat up and opened my book. He was still there.

"You know why I used to mess with you, Ella?

" 'Cause you're a jerk?"

"Naw. 'Cause I didn't like you. You had it all. Cool parents, your uncle Buddy, the barbershop guys. And *everybody* listened to you when you told those stupid stories. You were just some spoiled brat.

"But then, in the one-on-one, you pushed back. I liked that. Then there was the bold move with taking the movies. You got caught, but it was still bold. But now you're sitting here whining with some lame excuse that you don't like his movies so you're not going to the gala. Maybe I was right about you after all. You're just some spoiled kid who wants it all her way."

"But you didn't see it; it was just terrible! He made black people look like fools," I shouted.

"Then you need to be up front and ask him what the deal was, not just give up like a big baby."

My eyes were stinging as I watched him walk away. I could barely see through the tears.

I had always thought that I was better than Alphonso. First of all, he was a boy. Being a girl made me—I don't know, smarter than him. It was only natural. Then again, I felt pretty dumb right now, so maybe it wasn't so natural.

I did have a lot more than he did—two parents *plus* my uncle Buddy, a nice house—but I never even thought about it. So how could I act stuck-up? But maybe I did.

117

Maybe I was too used to having things go my way. All I knew was Alphonso was the one who had it all together, while I was acting like a big baby about the movies. But they were so . . . never mind what they were. I had to ask Uncle Buddy why he'd made them.

Ms. Sewall walked into the room, holding a small package.

"Here's an extra copy of the video you and Alphonso made. I kept the original to show at the gala. And here are the films for your Uncle Buddy. Thanks for delivering them for me, Ella." She handed me the package.

"You're welcome, Ms. Sewall," I said.

"I think I understand now," Ms. Sewall said, pointing to the cassette marked *Heavenly Hostess,* now in my hands. "If I were Mr. Jackson, I'd probably have done the same thing back then. Just given up, disappeared. My goodness, how it must have hurt him."

"What?" I spoke so loudly it sounded like I was yelling at Ms. Sewall. She told me to calm down.

But it was hard to calm down. I felt like I had 498 pieces of a jigsaw puzzle put together, but the last 2 pieces were lost somewhere under the furniture. I knew it had something to do with that grinning man and the angel and how bad it made me feel. Had Uncle Buddy told the man to act that way? Had Uncle Buddy stopped making movies because of something in *Heavenly Hostess*? I had to ask him, no matter how mad he might get. I had to know what it all meant.

SCENE 14

Pan: *The camera moves from left to right or vice versa, and up and down to show you how big something is. Pan is short for* panorama.

A terrific pan of a busy Columbia Road filled the screen.

I didn't know what I was going to say to Uncle Buddy when I got home, but I kept repeating to myself, "I've got to know, I've got to know." My stomach was in a knot and my backpack felt like it carried five bricks inside instead of just a few books and three little videotapes. Dad opened the door, and I just stood in the hallway.

"Take your coat off, Ella," he told me. He went into the kitchen to get dinner started.

I looked at the stairs going up to the second floor, to Uncle Buddy's room, and wished my personal rainbow was there.

"Ella?" my dad said. He looked down the hallway. "Why are you still standing there?"

"I've got to know."

"Know what?" he asked, throwing the dish towel over his shoulder.

The backpack was already halfway down my arms, and I let it slide down to the floor. I unzipped it, took the tapes out, and headed up the stairs, leaving my father without an answer.

"Hello, Ella," greeted Uncle Buddy when he saw me standing in the doorway of his room. He put down his book and opened his arms for my hug. I gave him a peck on the cheek. I wondered if he was going to be mad at me all over again if I asked. Maybe even madder than when I took the films without his permission.

I had to know.

I pulled up a chair and leaned in close. I held the package with the videotapes tight. Taking a deep breath, I plunged right in.

"Uncle Buddy, do you remember the first story you ever told me? I do. It was the story about Gertie Watkins leaving Dry Prong, Louisiana, with just her suitcase. She was trying to get to Chicago to get a good job and help out her family. So many things happened to her on the way that I thought she'd never get there. Every night you'd end it with her bumping into the next problem, and I couldn't wait to hear how she got out of it. She always did because she was a quick thinker. She finally got to Chicago and found a good job and sent for her family, and they came up north to get away from that mean man that owned their farm.

"The kids at school always like for me to tell them the westerns—*Wild Bill Pickett*, the gunfights, the posses. But my favorite is still the one about Gertie." I was talking really fast and my fingers were aching because I was holding the tapes so tight.

"What I want to know, Uncle Buddy . . . what I want to know is the story about the man and the angel. You never told me that one."

My eyes were stinging. I tried to hold back the tears, but I couldn't. They rolled down my face in long, straight lines. I concentrated on breathing quietly. Maybe if I didn't look up, he wouldn't notice that I was crying.

I felt him unfold my fingers from the tapes. I looked up.

"Come on downstairs," he said.

"I gave Ms. Sewall two movies to clean up. *Flames of Wrath* and *Heavenly Hostess*," began Uncle Buddy. He had called Mom and Dad into the family room, and we were all sitting side by side on the sofa. Uncle Buddy held up the videotapes. "I picked those particular two for a reason."

"*Flames of Wrath* shows you why I became a film-maker. I knew my movies could change the way the world looked at and thought about black people. The black people who came to see them used to break down and cry with happiness and relief to finally see themselves on-screen, acting like real people, with strengths and weak-nesses, rather than like buffoons and simpletons who existed only to give white people a laugh.

"But just a handful of Negroes were seeing my movies, and I was preaching to the choir, to those who already agreed with my point of view. Suppose *many* people could see my movies, whites *and* Negroes? I felt I could begin to chip away at some of the race hatred in America. Change the minds of white people who were just plain ignorant about black people. Open their eyes so they could see we were human, just like them.

"That's what I told myself, anyway. Somehow the glamour and money of Hollywood got all mixed up in that idea. Even though I thought I was going to Hollywood for the right reason, I later knew my own pride and ego had played a part, too. I wanted to be a big-time director that the whole world knew about—not just Negroes in the small southern towns and the black sections of Chicago and Detroit, where I had been showing my films."

Uncle Buddy paused. He put one of the tapes into the VCR.

"This is *Heavenly Hostess*. The first picture I made in Hollywood, and the last picture I ever made."

"Hollywood?" said Dad.

"I saw some envelopes addressed to you at a Hollywood address in the trunk! You made movies in Hollywood?" I asked.

"This," he said, pressing the play button, "will tell you why I turned away from filmmaking and never looked back."

The TV screen was dark, and then the large numbers—5, 4, 3, 2, 1—of the leader tape filled it. A lion roared. The man in the field and the angel appeared on the screen.

"Uncle Buddy?" Mom said with surprise.

"I don't understand," said Dad with a frown.

"When I went out to Hollywood," Uncle Buddy explained slowly, "I was part of the race division."

"Race division?" I asked.

"Hollywood was like a big department store. The race

division sold only Negro movies. This department hired Negro actors, singers, writers, directors, and me. They hired me."

"But Uncle Buddy, I know you wouldn't make a movie like this," said Dad.

"I didn't. They told me I'd be in charge. Hired my actors, Ella, Whitney, four or five others who had worked with me for years. I shot a good, thoughtful film about people's ideas of heaven and hell. They called me in, told me it was weak, and asked me to jazz it up.

"You know what that meant—making Negroes look childish and stupid. I told them I wouldn't do it. So they jazzed it up themselves and released it under my name. I walked."

"But *they* messed it up! It wasn't your fault," I yelled.

"First, let me tell you about the sin of pride. I knew before I went to Hollywood that they didn't respect Negro actors or directors. But I thought I was such a great talent that of course they would respect me. I *was* talented. But you can't change years of racism or the way people think. They didn't see my talent, they just saw the color of my skin.

"Second, what they did to my actors, who were like my family, hurt badly, Ella. We had already made almost

125

fifty movies together before we went to Hollywood. They made them shuffle and look ignorant in *Heavenly Hostess*. That hurt. But they also signed them to long-term contracts. Two or three of them spent the rest of their lives playing maids and butlers in all-white pictures. The others, disgusted, just left Hollywood, but they were barred from working in other films anywhere because of the contract.

"In my eyes I had failed, as a man and as a director. I couldn't protect them. I sold out and they paid for it."

"But what about the movies you made before you went to Hollywood?" I asked. "Why didn't you want people to see them?"

Uncle Buddy chuckled. "Now, those are good movies, but . . . how can I explain?"

He got up and went to the bookshelf where my mom had framed one of the valentine cards I had made for her in kindergarten.

"Suppose I decided to show this to everybody at your sixth-grade graduation? To show them what a fine artist you are?"

"What!" I laughed, embarrassed. "Uncle Buddy! That would be silly. I can draw much better than that now."

"Well, that's my point. I was nineteen years old when I

made those movies. By the time I got to Hollywood in 1935, I was doing work that was much better. So they just seemed too . . . I don't know . . . just not my best work. So they didn't seem important."

"But they're great! You know that, don't you?"

"Yes, baby, thanks to you, you stubborn little thing!"

"Besides," said Dad, "you still must love movies, because you take Ella every week, without fail, to the matinees."

"Took me about twenty years to walk back into a movie theater. And oh, the changes. The color, the sound, the special effects! Made my movies really seem like a lifetime ago. And then when I looked at this," he said, picking up the other tape, "I saw the future."

I thought the other tape he was holding was *Flames of Wrath*. I was really surprised when he popped the other videocassette into the VCR, and it was our class project! The first card came up, and we heard the music from "As Time Goes By." The words "You must remember this, a kiss is just a kiss" serenaded us as a terrific pan of a busy Columbia Road filled the screen.

The sights and sounds of Jackson's Barbershop filled the screen for the next eight minutes. Every now and then Uncle Buddy would mutter, "Uh-huh, uh-huh," in

127

agreement, or laugh at a particular shot or phrase. When the film was finished, everyone was silent.

"Ella, that was excellent," Dad said finally.

My heart was pounding so hard I could hardly hear my own thoughts. "Thank you, Dad," I said.

For the first time in my life I knew I had a really important, grown-up thought, and I knew I was right, and if I could gather enough breath to push the words out, I was going to say it.

"Taking Uncle Buddy's movies was the worst thing I've ever done in my whole life. I deserved all the punishments you gave me. But I think we should all go to the gala.

"Uncle Buddy belongs there. I think it was wrong for Uncle Buddy to stop making movies just because he was ashamed of what happened.

"After you found out I took his movies, I wanted to just forget about filmmaking, too. But now I think I shouldn't stop just because I'm ashamed of what I did."

I looked at Uncle Buddy. His eyes were watery. "Well, all right."

My parents looked at each other.

"You're right," Dad said with a slow smile.

128

I jumped up and threw my arms tightly around my mother and hugged first her, then Dad.

"Uncle Buddy," I said to him as I squeezed him last of all, "the world is waiting to meet Mr. W. B. Jackson."

SCENE 15

Credits: *At the opening and closing of the movie is a list of the people who helped complete the project: the director, writer, actors, camera operators, musicians, costumes, stunt people, makeup artists, even the people who brought lunch to the cast and crew every day.*

When the last line of the opening credits appeared on the screen, WRITTEN, PRODUCED, AND DIRECTED BY W. B. JACKSON, *the applause grew louder . . .*

You would think it was Academy Awards night!" my mom exclaimed.

I rolled down the backseat passenger window to get a better look up the street at all the lights and at the long red carpet that extended up the stairs to the entrance of the Baird Auditorium. People were dressed up and looked like stars in black suits, lacy dresses, kente cloth, and sparkly jewelry. I couldn't wait to get out there!

Unfortunately, we were stuck in a traffic jam on Constitution Avenue—me, Mom, Dad, and Uncle

Buddy—and there were no parking spaces, either.

"I'll try circling the block again," Dad announced. He didn't sound too hopeful.

"Honey," Mom began. "Maybe we could just let Ella and Uncle Buddy out, and we'll join them later. They could get seats for us."

"Yeah!" I shouted. I was getting frantic sitting in the backseat, waiting to get there, wanting to be there so bad! Uncle Buddy patted my hand. "Calm down, Sugar," he said. Then he adjusted his collar and tie. "You sure this looks okay? It's been in storage for a while. Does it smell like mothballs?"

"No," my mom answered. I leaned over and sniffed his shoulder just in case. All I could smell was aftershave and just a little hair tonic—the kind he used every day in his barbershop.

"You look very handsome," added Dad.

"Yeah, like a penguin," I said with a giggle.

We drove around the block again. Still no parking!

"Let's go!" I shouted, reaching for the door latch. Uncle Buddy stopped me and made me look before getting out of the car.

"Come on, we're late!" I cried, and we started up the red carpet to the doors.

131

We were right outside the theater, and I could hear the people inside applauding. It sure sounded crowded! Then, suddenly, it was quiet.

Uncle Buddy opened the door very slowly, and I poked my head in to see what was going on.

Ms. Sewall was onstage, adjusting the microphone at the podium.

"Great!" I whispered over my shoulder to Uncle Buddy. "I think it's just starting!"

Uncle Buddy opened the door all the way and took my hand. He didn't move, though. He just stood there, holding my hand, looking kind of strange.

"What's the matter, Uncle Buddy?" I noticed that his hand felt a little cold and sweaty.

"Nothing. Just a bit nervous."

"Don't be nervous. I'm here," I reassured him. He smiled at me, and the strange look went away. We walked into the auditorium.

We were standing at the back when Ms. Sewall began her speech. There was a big *whoop* noise that made the audience laugh. When it stopped, Ms. Sewall began again.

"I'd like to welcome all of you to our gala celebration benefit for the Bancroft Media Arts Center. I am Ricki

132

Sewall, filmmaker, historian and, recently, teacher. It makes me very happy to see so many faces out there, because that means you understand and support the importance of art and culture in our society. . . ."

I felt someone tugging my sleeve. I looked over and there was Alphonso.

"I knew you'd show up," he said.

He pulled at the lapels of his suit—thinking he looked real good, I guess—and waved at Uncle Buddy.

"Looking good, Mr. Jackson."

"Thanks, Alphonso. You, too."

"What about me?" I asked. After all, I don't wear lacy dresses every day.

"You look okay," Alphonso said. I was surprised to hear him say something nice. I couldn't help but smile.

"Well, it's about time," Uncle Buddy whispered. "I'm glad to see you two finally getting along."

I was glad, too. Alphonso put up with a lot of crabbing from me. Still, every time I asked him for help, he was there.

"Thanks, Alphonso. You were right about just asking Uncle Buddy about the movie with the angel. He explained everything."

"Well," said Alphonso, taking his turn, "you *did* help me get that A. And Mrs. Henderson wrote on my report

133

card that my behavior was better because I had a 'focus.' I guess that was because of you. *And* our movie. So, thanks."

Alphonso held out his hand. I honestly didn't know why for a second. Then I realized: He wanted to shake my hand.

I reached out, hoping he wouldn't do something dumb like pinch me or pull back real quick. He just shook my hand. It was cool. Way cool.

Uncle Buddy glanced down at us and gave us the thumbs-up sign.

We had missed the part of Ms. Sewall's speech about the importance of arts and society. I could tell now she was going to start talking about Uncle Buddy! Yippee!

"Something wonderful has happened. Because of my project at Bancroft, and because of the tenacious spirit of one of my students . . ."

"She means me!" I said, too loudly. A few parents in the back row turned around to look at me and smile.

"I came face-to-face with a legend. A man I believed was no longer with us. A man whose talent was way ahead of his time. He has graciously consented to letting us view a bit of his work tonight. I had originally hoped he could be here to share in this rediscovery with all of us—"

I began to jump up and down, waving my arms to get

134

Ms. Sewall's attention. She couldn't see me, probably because of the bright lights above the stage.

Mom and Dad walked in just then.

"Ella," Dad asked, "what are you trying to do?"

"I'm trying to let Ms. Sewall know we're here!" I told him, still waving.

"Why don't you just go on down to the stage?"

"I'll go!" Alphonso cried.

"No, I'll go!" I said.

"Why don't you both go?" suggested Uncle Buddy.

Alphonso and I took off running down the aisle. As we got closer, Ms. Sewall finally saw us. She leaned over the edge of the stage.

"What's going on?" she asked.

"Uncle Buddy is here!"

"Here? Now?"

"Yes!"

"Will he come up to the stage?"

"If you ask him to, he will," I told her.

I looked back up the aisle at Mom, Dad, and Uncle Buddy and nodded.

"Ella, Alphonso, come up to the podium. I want to introduce you, too."

My heart started pounding really hard. I looked at all

135

the faces in the audience and suddenly my knees felt weak.

"Come on," urged Alphonso.

"I don't think I can walk up there!"

"Don't be stupid," Alphonso cried. "Here, hold my hand."

Alphonso took my hand and pulled me up the steps to the stage. We walked over to the podium and stood waiting for whatever Ms. Sewall was going to do.

"Ladies and gentlemen," Ms. Sewall began, "I have a wonderful surprise for you. As I was saying, I was going to show you some of the works of W. B. Jackson—but perhaps you'd like to *meet* him first. Mr. Jackson?"

The audience was filled with people we knew from the neighborhood. I could hear them whispering, "Buddy Jackson, you mean *our* Buddy Jackson? He made movies?" Everyone turned to look back at the same time.

Uncle Buddy slowly began to walk down the aisle. He was just like a king coming to get his crown and purple robe. The audience started applauding, then cheering, then jumping to their feet.

I wasn't nervous anymore. My heart was singing! Uncle Buddy looked so wonderful, waving to the audience as he came to the podium. He shook hands with Ms. Sewall and gave her a little kiss on the cheek. Then he hugged Alphonso. When he came to me, he looked me right in the eyes and said, "Thank you." Then he hugged me.

"Hey, stupid," Alphonso whispered to me. "You're supposed to be happy."

I didn't know what he was talking about, until I realized I was crying. I'd seen Mom cry when she was happy, and I'd never understood why. Now I did. As I watched Uncle Buddy with the spotlight on him, I couldn't help smiling and crying at the same time.

Then Uncle Buddy turned to the podium. A hush fell over the audience.

He stood there for a moment, not sure what to say. I reached up and squeezed his hand. He smiled.

"Thank you, ladies and gentlemen, for that warm reception. A long time ago, when I was a very young man, I had a dream, a dream it took half a century to realize. And it is only because of the stubbornness of my loving grandniece, Ella Jackson, that I am here tonight. Ella, Alphonso Green, and all the children in Ms. Sewall's class are tomorrow's filmmakers."

Alphonso held up a hand and I gave him a big high-five.

"For a long time, I felt that this part of my life was best

137

left closed. Ella helped me to see that I was wrong. I told her she was a girl and girls couldn't make movies. Again Ella helped me see I was wrong. That's her job, and the job of every young person we have in our lives—to keep us thinking, to make us come up with honest answers.

"When I looked at the film she did for her class project, I saw how proud she was not of W. B. Jackson, the director, but of me, Buddy Jackson, the best darn barber on Columbia Road. And that's when I realized that I needed to share my past and my work with her and, I guess, with you all as well.

"There is a big lesson to be learned here. And that is, we all have dreams, longings, ambitions. Listen to your hearts. Follow your dreams. Don't give up, don't compromise. Don't let 'no' mean 'you can't.' 'No' just means you have to find another way to do it. That's what Ella taught me.

"Well, enough talking. Let's start the movie. I hope you like it."

The audience cheered. It was the most incredible thing I ever heard!

Slowly the lights began to dim. Uncle Buddy grabbed my hand and said, "Quick, let's find seats."

We found Mom and Dad sitting with Alphonso's mom, and they'd saved three seats for us. Everyone was hugging and kissing, and strangers were reaching over to shake Uncle Buddy's hand.

And then it was dark. Since no one could see me, I took that moment to close my eyes and breathe a sigh of relief. Everything had turned out okay. My dishonesty could have ruined everything. I had been very lucky, but it had taken a lot of love for Uncle Buddy to forgive me. I wanted to remember this incredible moment forever.

Up on the screen flashed the title, *Flames of Wrath*. Everyone began to applaud. I couldn't help but giggle, and under my breath I said, "Gertie Watkins got off the train with only one beat-up suitcase. . . ."

Ella DuChamps appeared on the screen—bigger than life and totally a star. She was walking down the street as if she owned it. And then, when the last line of the opening credits appeared on the screen, WRITTEN, PRODUCED, AND DIRECTED BY W. B. JACKSON, the applause grew louder, and people began to whistle and call out Uncle Buddy's name.

"That's for you!" I shouted. I looked up at Uncle Buddy, and he was smiling the biggest smile ever.